Forever with Him

Also by Sofia Tate

Breathless for Him
Devoted to Him

Forever with Him

SOFIA TATE

New York Boston

Forever Yours
Hachette Book Group
1290 Avenue of the Americas
New York, NY 10104
hachettebookgroup.com
twitter.com/foreverromance

First published as an ebook and as a print on demand: August 2015

Forever Yours is an imprint of Grand Central Publishing.
The Forever Yours name and logo are trademarks of Hachette Book Group, Inc.

The publisher is not responsible for websites (or their content) that are not owned by the publisher.

The Hachette Speakers Bureau provides a wide range of authors for speaking events. To find out more, go to www.hachettespeakersbureau.com or call (866) 376-6591.

ISBN: 978-1-4555-3507-1

For my sister, Taissa
I am so proud of you. You are an amazing mom and watching
you with Kvitka, I see Mama reflected in you. I love having you
as my sister, knowing that you have my back no matter what.
I'm glad that we're now best friends and our hair-pulling,
scratching, and biting days are behind us!

For my brother, David
Confession time from your oldest sister—I've always been
envious of you, marching to the beat of your own drum
and not caring what anyone else thinks. You are always
there for Mama, Taissa, Kvitka, and me, for which I am
eternally grateful. Now you have found the lovely
Liana, and I am over the moon for the both of you.
You deserve it, and so much more.

For my grandmother Nancy Bushnell
You have always been more than a grandmother to me—a
second mom, confidante, older sister, and best friend all rolled
up into one dazzling combination with a side order of tough
love when necessary. Thank you for taking such good care of
me. I'm so proud to be your number one (as ever, in age only,
not importance).

Acknowledgments

I have come to the end of my journey with my beloveds, Davison and Allegra. I can't believe I'm writing the acknowledgments for their final story. Time has flown by so quickly, and it's been an amazing experience for me. I'm grateful beyond words that the person who guided me during my first publishing experience was my rock-star editor extraordinaire, Megha Parekh. Thank you, Megha, for your endless patience and support and taking such good care of Davison and Allegra. I have learned so much from you, knowledge that I will always carry with me. We still have Tomas and Lucy's story to tell, and I can't wait to start working on it with you!

My eternal gratitude to the amazing team at Forever Romance/ Grand Central Publishing, who has always been there for me, and as a debut author, knowing I had your support meant the world to me! Leah Hultenschmidt, you are so lovely and encouraging, and as a new author, I'm so thankful for that. Julie Paulauski, my amazing publicist: from our first conversation, I knew you would do everything you could for Davison and Allegra—you have, and

I adore you for it. My boundless gratitude also to Jodi Rosoff, Marissa Sangiacomo, Janet Robbins for catching all of my typos, and Elizabeth Turner for the beautiful covers (I think *Forever with Him* might be my favorite!).

To my Forever Romance pub buddies: Kennedy Ryan—24/7/365. LOVE! Lia Riley—you are a diamond in a sea of cubic zirconia! I'll never forget our afternoon in the East Village with GGB! Eliza Freed, Shannon Richard, Jessica Lemmon, Chelsea Fine, Lauren Smith, Shelley Coriell, Rie Warren—rock stars, one and all! And to Cecilia Tan—your blurbs and support for *Breathless for Him* meant the world to me! I can't wait to be your book fair signing neighbor!

Linda Judge, my BFF from Buckinghamshire: my rock. The one who holds the key to the vault. If we ever ceased being friends, I'd be in massive trouble. But I know that will never happen. #bestmatesforlife

Holly Wright: my soul sister. No words are ever necessary.

Logan Belle: thank goodness for you. That's all I can say without becoming too emotional.

Katana Collins, K.M. Jackson, Julia Tagan, and Felice Stevens: extra-mushy thanks!

Autumn at Agents of Romance: what a joy it was to finally meet you at RT! You are so amazing and lovely! Thank you so much for your support and friendship! Having you in my life is a true gift.

Karen Mandeville-Steer: my beautiful TimTam enabler! Thank you for filling in the holes with D&A! You are a rock star!

Jane Tara: the planets were in perfect alignment when I made the decision to come to ARRC2015 and was seated with you at our signing table. You are gorgeous inside and out and words cannot adequately express how grateful I am to know you and be able to call you a friend.

Rachael Johns: your words move me and your selfless spirit inspires me. #mutuallovesociety

Amy Almond: I promised you a public acknowledgment of my gratitude to you for turning me on to *How to Get Away with Murder*. And now, I have one word for you in return: *Outlander*.

To my family and friends: thank you for being there for me when I need you and for understanding when I need to be a hermit in my writing cave.

I need to create a BLOGGERS RULE! T-shirt because it is you, you wonderful group of book lovers, who played an enormous role in spreading the word about Davison and Allegra and making sure the world knew about them. All of the countless hours you have spent reading and writing about my beloveds have not gone unnoticed or unappreciated by me, and I hope to meet every single one of you (if I haven't already) in person someday to thank you for everything you've done for D&A and me!

I save my final words of acknowledgment to all of the beautiful readers who embraced Davison and Allegra and joined me on their journey wherever they took us. I am so grateful for you, for your reviews, your e-mails, your comments, your tweets, and for the time you have given them. I gave D&A the HEA they deserve because it is for you that I made sure they got it. THANK YOU!!!

Love, Sofia xoxo

Forever with Him

Chapter 1

Allegra

Watching my fiancé, Davison Cabot Berkeley, standing in front of the mirror in his walk-in closet adjusting his bow tie while wearing a custom-tailored black tuxedo is an exercise in torture.

Exquisite torture.

He stands ramrod straight, his emerald eyes, full of determination and focus, practically etching a mark in the glass. His chiseled jaw is locked. He wants to look perfect, and all I want to do is rip off the tie, pull apart his pristine white tuxedo shirt, sending its buttons scattering across the closet floor like pebbles, slam my lips over his, and plunge my tongue into his mouth. Then, once his broad, muscled chest presents itself to me, I'll run my tongue and hands over it down to the bulge enveloped in the soft, silky fabric of his trousers, unzip them, and sink to the carpet until my knees hit as I take his hot, velvety cock into my mouth and…

"If you don't stop ogling me like that, Venus, I'll have no choice but to fuck you right here in this closet."

His declaration snaps me back to the present, which works so effortlessly when he says it, addressing me with his preferred nickname for me, and with that low rumble in his voice that makes me wet at the sound of it.

"I didn't realize you saw me standing here."

He pivots to me to stare at me full-on. "Baby, I don't have to see you to know you're near me. I just *know*."

I smile. "Goes both ways, Harvard."

His eyes warm at the sound of the term of endearment I use only for him. "Come here," his voice beckons, my pussy aching at the sound of his insistence.

I step over to him. He positions me in front of the mirror with him behind me, his warm breath in my ear.

Finally, after a pause, I hear him take in a breath. He runs his hands over my dress, a deep red strapless gown that matches the ruby ring I always wear on my right hand, the one Davison gave me in Venice when we rode under the Bridge of Sighs in the gondola.

"God, you're so beautiful. How did I get so fucking lucky?" he murmurs in my ear, gripping my body tightly to his.

"What can I say? You're a very good boy."

The warmth of his lips descends on my neck as his mouth begins to suck softly on my flesh. "Ha! Hardly!" he mumbles under his breath.

My head lolls back onto his shoulder, savoring the feel of his touch. "Hmm, you might have a point there."

I can feel his heartbeat increasing against my back. My core clenches as I grow more aroused with each pull of his lips on my neck. His hands roam over my chest, holding my breasts in his hands. His body vibrates behind me in a low moan as his thumbs stroke my nipples, which instantly harden under my dress.

The sound of a phone pinging in the bedroom forces Davison to pull away, both of us groaning in annoyance.

I sigh. "I think it's mine."

Davison follows me back into the bedroom and watches over my shoulder as I pick up my phone, grunting his annoyance. "Christ, can't he leave you alone for two seconds?"

I exhale in exasperation as I watch him pick up his wallet and phone from the nightstand. "We have to leave in five minutes," he announces.

"I'm ready," I reply to his retreating back. "Just give me a sec."

The text is from Jared Saxon, my new manager. After I was one of the winners of the Metropolitan Opera National Council auditions a few months ago, Jared signed me on as a client soon after. He's managed opera singers for almost twenty years, from divas to newcomers. I spoke with Ginevra Ventura, or La Diva as she's better known, the international opera star with whom I apprenticed over the summer, before I signed on with him. Even though he wasn't her manager, she said that he had a solid reputation in the business, which was good enough for me. My professional singing career since then has taken off. Because of him, I was offered the chance to audition at the Met, and then starring in the role I've been dreaming of for as long as I've known I wanted to be an opera singer became a reality—the lead role of Mimi in *La Bohème*.

Ever since then, my life has been a whirlwind. Between rehearsals and meetings with Jared and his team, I haven't had much time with Papa and Lucy. It's been somewhat easier with Davison because as of two months ago, we are now living together. Even though he spends what feels like every waking hour working with his new company, The DCB Group, I still get to see him every night when he comes to bed and every morning when I open my eyes.

I swipe my phone open to read Jared's text.

I'll be waiting for you when you arrive. There will be a press line, so make sure you get lots of solo shots with the paps without Davison. I also suggest that you wear your hair down. See you there. J

Ugh.

Jared has done such amazing things for my career, and I never would've been given the opportunities I've had since he started managing me, but there's a fine line between managing and dictating. Plus, there is no way in hell I'm taking my hair out of the chignon that took me ages to get right. My career is one thing—my hair, that's off-limits.

* * *

"Did he say when he'd call, Ian? Okay, tell him I'll be in the office tomorrow at nine, so we can set up a conference call then. Anything else?"

I glance over at Davison on his cell, then at his left hand as he holds my right one, sitting in the Maybach on our way up the West Side Highway. This is something that he recently started doing. He's on the phone now much more, but even though he's talking to someone else, he always has to maintain a connection with me, whether it's holding my hand or curving his arm around my shoulders.

Davison is the man who mesmerized me from the moment I met him and still does, so much that sometimes I'm still overwhelmed with the intensity of the love he has for me and the one I have for him.

That love has put us through the wringer. Our journey to where we are now, engaged to be married, was waylaid numerous times, from Davison's ex-girlfriend Ashton Canterbury's attempt to keep us apart, then my kidnap nightmare with the scum, Carlo Morandi, who murdered my mother in front of me when I was five years old, and finally, the event that changed me forever: Davison being shot in the shoulder before he and his father were to meet with the Feds about the crimes the elder Berkeley had committed.

When Davison was lying on the ground with his blood spilling out of him onto the concrete, I'd never felt more useless in my life, and more than that, I knew that if he died, I would lose myself, the self that Davison brought out in me. The me that is now more confident, more open, less afraid, with more love than I ever had before in my life.

But he survived, and now we were going to start a life together. And I've never been happier in my life.

Tonight is one of the most important events in the Manhattan social calendar—the opening-night gala of the new season at the Metropolitan Opera. I always watched the excitement from across the street before I started my night shift at Le Bistro as a coat-check girl—limos and town cars pulling up to the plaza in front of the Met, a huge screen set up to broadcast the arrivals and the opera itself, the shouts from the paparazzi calling out celebrity names, the flashes from their cameras lighting up the night sky. And now, I'm going to be walking that red carpet with my fiancé as a contracted singer with the Metropolitan Opera. I'm still amazed at it all, but even more, I'm humbled and grateful.

As Charles pulls the Maybach over to the curb, I spot the red carpet for the arrivals spread out elegantly across the wide stairs, the photographers caged behind metal barriers. And at the near edge waiting for me checking his phone is Jared with a petite blonde.

Davison groans under his breath. He's spotted Jared as well. "Who's that with him?"

"I have no idea. He wants me to get solo shots with the paps."

"Of course he does," he murmurs, still looking out the window.

I tug on Davison's hand. "Harvard."

He turns and looks me directly in the eye.

"I love you."

A smile breaks across his face. He runs his fingers down my face and leans in for a quick kiss. "I love you too, baby."

"Do I look okay?" I ask, touching my hair gently to make sure it's stayed in place.

He takes my hand and kisses it. "Silly fiancée." He hands me my clutch purse, the one that belonged to my late mother that I always took with me to the opera like she did when she was alive, then wraps the black vintage fringed shawl I bought at a little boutique in the East Village around my shoulders. "Come on, Venus. Time to put our game faces on."

I nod and take my purse from him. As per our routine, I wait for Davison to exit his side of the car to come around and open my door. He helps me out of the Maybach, and instantly, we're blinded by exploding flashbulbs and our names being called out to gain our attention.

Jared immediately appears at my side with the blonde right behind him.

"Finally," he huffs in exasperation. "What took you so long?"

"It's called traffic, Saxon," Davison barks at him, his grip on my hand akin to a steel vise.

I press my thumb into Davison's fingers in an attempt to calm him. Honestly, I don't mind when Davison is protective and territorial over me, but because Jared is the man who manages my budding opera career, I need to maintain a healthy working relationship with him, as much as it kills Davison sometimes.

"This is Alicia," Jared announces, completely ignoring Davison and gesturing to the blonde. "She's going to help you work the press line. Just make sure you get the solo shots in front of the step and repeat."

Alicia nods. "Of course, Jared. This way, Miss Orsini."

I barely have time to assure Jared I'll be fine before Davison pulls on my hand and deliberately walks in front of Alicia, ignoring the woman's pleas to wait for her. He walks with me up the stairs at a slow yet determined pace since I'm wearing stilettos.

Once we reach the top of the stairs, the paparazzi begin to scream our names again for our attention. Thankfully, Davison is an old pro at this, a former Manhattan bachelor and permanent fixture on Page Six. He guides me down the red carpet, his hand holding mine tightly, pausing now and then so the press can get pictures. Alicia shadows us, keeping a few feet behind.

We arrive at the backdrop with the logo of the Met and the evening's sponsors emblazoned on it when Alicia steps forward. "We need a few shots of Allegra alone, Mr. Berkeley."

Davison smiles while clenching his jaw. "Certainly."

Alicia steps aside, but not before Davison takes my face in his hands and kisses me long and deep. Hoots and catcalls rise up from the photographers.

When he pulls away, a sly, knowing smirk appears on his face, and I know exactly what he's feeling because my face mirrors his. Without words, he's telling me *You're mine*, and a wave of warmth envelops my entire body.

I watch as he takes a few steps away, and I turn back to the cameras.

"Show us the ring, Allegra!" one photographer shouts.

I smile widely as I raise my left hand and proudly hold up my ring, which once belonged to Davison's grandmother, to the lenses aimed at it.

I pose for a few more minutes when I sense Davison next to me, his hand taking mine again into his tight grip.

He turns to the cameras and smiles. "Thank you, everyone."

Alicia appears from the side. "She still needs—"

I shake my head. "I'm staying with Davison now, Alicia. And I apologize in advance if that upsets Jared."

With Davison pulling me tightly into him, I throw my shoulders back and let him guide me into the building.

After we show our tickets, a voice shouts at me across the crowded space. "Alli!"

I smile as I watch my best friend, Luciana Gibbons, or Lucy, as I call her, approach us, a flute of champagne in her hand. She looks gorgeous in an ice-blue gown that perfectly matches her eyes and a pair of silver slingbacks on her feet, as she takes turns embracing us both.

Lucy's eyes are shining with pure joy. "Did you see? Did you see?"

"See what?" I ask cluelessly. "We just got here."

She thrusts the program at us, open to a page in the middle. "Look! Isn't he gorgeous?"

Davison and I glance down at the picture of Lucy's boyfriend, Tomas Novotny, in the cast list. He's singing a supporting role in the opening-night production of Wagner's *Das Rheingold*, and while I'm thrilled for him, I wouldn't be surprised to hear Lucy had shouted the news from the rooftops, which as a proud girlfriend, would entirely be her prerogative.

We both nod. "Yes, he is very handsome," I agree.

Lucy snatches the program back from us. "'Handsome'? He's fucking hot!"

"Indeed," Davison adds drily, which makes me bite back a laugh. "We should get to our seats."

I lean in and hug Lucy again. "If I don't see you at intermission, you're coming over this week so we can finalize the wedding plans, right?"

"Of course. Your maid of dishonor will not let you down."

"Well, if the name fits..."

"Which it does," she agrees.

"I should get you a T-shirt with that printed on it," I offer.

"Which I can wear for your bachelorette party."

Davison clears his throat. "Okay, now we really have to go. And, by the way, Luciana, there will be no bachelorette party. If you must, throw us an engagement party if you are desperate for something to do."

Uh-oh. Open mouth, insert foot, Harvard.

I can already see the wheels spinning in Lucy's mind thanks to her light blue eyes, now illuminated brightly in excitement.

"And if you have a bachelorette party," Davison continues, "you'll be wearing high-necked dresses with long gloves, sipping tea, and eating cookies without some naked man shaking his junk in my fiancée's face."

As he pulls me away, Lucy yells behind us, "Don't be a party pooper, Money Boy!"

I cringe at the sound of Lucy's nickname for Davison, one he loathes.

"She just had to yell that across the floor on opening night at the Met, didn't she?" he grumbles under his breath, his warm hand firmly placed on the small of my back.

I quickly peck him on the cheek. "I'll make sure to ease the pain for you later, baby."

His hot breath caresses my ear. "How long is this opera again?"

* * *

The elevator to our apartment opens, emitting a soft *ding*. Davison steps through the doors with me.

"You can put me down now, Harvard," I point out to him.

My stilettos hanging from one of my hands and the other coiled around his neck, Davison carries me across to the living room, kisses me on the forehead, and lays me down on the couch.

He gives me a soft smile. "The usual?"

"Yes, please."

My head falls back onto the cushions. I hear ice clinking in the kitchen. When I look up again, Davison comes out of the kitchen holding my Baileys over ice and his Scotch neat.

My heart stops at the sight of him.

"Wait," I ask of him.

His eyebrows furrow in confusion. "What?"

My eyes roam over his body. His bow tie is undone, curling around his tight neck, and his tuxedo shirt is open a few buttons, revealing his bare, hard chest underneath. With his dark hair tousled after a long night, the man is sex personified. I purse my lips to keep myself in control, my insides clenching in anticipation of what is to come shortly. *More like* who *is to come.*

Fuck.

I shut my eyes, my cheeks flaming in hunger when I hear ice being shaken in front of my face.

I look up into my fiancé's hungry green eyes, taking the glass from him. "Thank you," I whisper.

Davison takes a swig of the amber liquid, puts it down on the coffee table, then picks up my legs, placing himself on the couch with my feet in his lap. I stretch out when he takes my feet in his hands and begins to massage them, just like he did in the Maybach during the drives home after the night shift at Le Bistro when we were dating.

"Mmmm, that feels amazing," I moan.

"Nice to know I haven't lost my touch."

"You never will, baby," I assure him.

Silence permeates the room as I enjoy his ministrations to my aching feet.

"Allegra?"

"Hmmm…"

"I know we've talked about this before, but Jared—"

I shake my head and sigh. "Oh, Davison, please don't start. I know what you're going to say…"

"It's not that I don't appreciate what he's done for your career, but I don't like the way he treats you."

"The only way he treats me is like a client," I counter.

"Look at me, Venus."

When I glance up at him, his eyes are grave and serious.

"The text he sent you unnerved me. Not that he was meeting you there, but the comment about your hair. I think he imagines himself as some kind of Svengali."

"Davison, that's ridiculous. And if you haven't noticed, I didn't take my hair down like he asked me to."

He nods. "That's true. But I just want you to promise me that if he does anything that makes you uncomfortable, you'll tell me and not hide it from me."

Fear and concern cross his beautiful deep green eyes, my heart breaking at the sight of it. I instantly know what he's thinking of—the time when I didn't tell him about Carlo Morandi's henchman, Tony, stalking me until he'd done the deed and kidnapped me.

I sit up, crawling over to Davison where I straddle his lap, hiking my dress up to my thighs. I take his face in my hands, cupping his chiseled jaw, running my thumbs over his cheeks.

"Harvard, I swear that if anything happens, if he does anything at all that can be considered over the line, I will tell you right away. Okay?"

"Okay," he whispers.

I smile at my fiancé as I lean in closer to him. "Now that we've cleared that up, I believe I made you a promise earlier this evening."

Davison raises his eyebrows in recognition. "Ah yes. You were going to ease my pain about Luciana's uncouth remark."

I take the bow tie from around his neck and hurl it behind my shoulder with a smirk. He grins at me wickedly as I start to unbutton his shirt, running my hands over his broad chest and hard muscles.

I place my mouth on him, licking his nipples, inhaling his scent of spice and sweat that intoxicated me from the start. Pure Davison.

"So good, Venus," he groans. "Always so fucking good."

I pull back and whisper, "I'm only getting started, baby. So just sit back and enjoy."

I slowly climb down from his lap to get to my feet. His eyes never leave mine as I unzip my dress, letting it fall to the floor in a rustle of silk. I'm left standing in my garter belt and stockings.

I watch with a greedy grin as a bulge appears in his trousers.

"No underwear," he growls. "You're killing me."

"Don't die on me yet, Davison. I've got one more thing to do before we declare your time of death and tag your toe."

I sink to my knees and quickly undo his zipper. His long, hard cock is hot in my hands and velvet to the touch. Screw the touching. I get right down to business and take his length into my mouth, sucking on it and instantly tasting the precum on the tip. I pump the base as I speed up my mouth.

"Oh God! Fuck, baby…"

My heart begins to race. It doesn't take long as his muscles lock and he bursts inside my mouth. I swallow the warm liquid, letting it ooze down my throat.

I quickly wipe my mouth on the back of my hand. He exhales loudly. "Get those gorgeous tits up here, baby. I need to return the favor for you."

I gasp excitedly in greedy anticipation as I jump up from the floor and hurl myself into his lap. Before I can settle myself in, he grabs my mouth and plunges his tongue inside me while simultaneously roughly kneading my breasts. The elegant, dashing public visage of Davison Cabot Berkeley has dissipated. In its place is a sex god intent on ravaging me.

I lock my ankles around his calves to anchor myself. His mouth rips away from mine and clamps itself onto my left breast, biting and licking and sucking. One hand goes around my waist, and the other begins stroking me, thrusting inside me over and over.

"Yes, Venus. Always so wet. So fucking wet," he groans.

"You do that to me, baby," I pant. "Only you."

His dexterous fingers find my clit, rubbing it hard. I'm going to come and it's going to be glorious. I ride Davison's skilled hand to the brink when I come, shuddering in such exquisite release.

I fall onto his chest, spent and sated. I glance up to see him begin to suck the fingers on his right hand, tasting my essence.

"Did I get rid of all of the pain for you?" I murmur under my breath.

He tips my chin up with his index finger and shakes his head, wincing as if he were still hurt. "Not all of it."

I turn my lips down, giving him a sad face. "Oh no. I should probably see to that."

Suddenly, he turns me around and scoops me up, rising to his feet with me in his arms.

"Indeed you should. But I think we'll need more room so I can have a full recovery."

I laugh out loud as he smiles back at me and hurries down the hallway to our bedroom, carrying me in his arms.

Chapter 2

Davison

I understand, but if you could just allow me to explain... Your concerns are completely valid, but I'm not investing your money, I'm merely telling you where to invest it... Of course. Thank you for your time. Good day, sir."

I place the phone back in its cradle on my desk. I look over at Ian Parker, sitting across from me in my office, the Bulldog from Yale who worked for me at my family's former company, Berkeley Holdings.

"Sorry. I thought he was a shoo-in," Ian offers in apology.

I shrug my shoulders in reply. "It's fine. Nothing we haven't encountered before. I think I need to get new business cards that say *THE DCB GROUP—I AM NOT MY FATHER* or something to that effect."

"You sure you don't want to hire a publicist?"

I shake my head. "Absolutely not. We don't need one. My name is famous enough. I want the company to grow by word of mouth, not some artificial spin."

"Okay. Just thought I'd throw it out there." He checks his watch. "Shit. I've got to meet someone for lunch in twenty minutes."

"Business or pleasure?"

I can't help but notice his mouth instantly widening into a smile at the question. "Definitely pleasure."

"Seeing someone new?"

He gives me a grin. "Yeah. It sort of came out of nowhere, but so far, so good."

"That's great, man. Come see me when you get back so we can strategize."

"Will do."

Once he walks out, I rise from my chair and stretch my back. I take in the look of my new office.

After Berkeley Holdings was declared insolvent, I decided I wanted a clean slate for my company. I wanted something more modern, in a building built in the present century, not the nineteenth. I found the perfect office space in a new high-rise that had just gone up in the Financial District. I was still in the hub of Wall Street, just without the baggage of the past. There are no brown leather chairs, no paintings of horses or hunting dogs on the walls. My office now evokes the look of a twenty-first-century business firm, not a room at the Harvard Club, a place I know too well since my blood runs Crimson.

With the walls painted in light gray, the furniture is all black, from the bookshelves and my desk to the credenza and chairs. The one splash of bright color is the Canaletto hanging on a near wall. It's of the Grand Canal in Venice, the city where Allegra and I had spent a glorious break away from everyone after she'd been rescued from Morandi, finding our way back to each other again.

But by far, the best part is the view from my office because I can see my apartment building, the one where Allegra now lives with me permanently.

Knowing how old-school her father is, I was worried about how it would go over with him—the idea of his only child, his daughter, moving in with a man without being married first. Just to add to that, I neglected one major part of the proposal—asking him for his daughter's hand in marriage. But as traditional as he is, after everything he and I went through together when Carlo Morandi kidnapped Allegra, cementing the bond between us when he saw how much I truly loved Allegra, he knew I was worthy of her. And so all of the worry had been for nothing because he had already seen firsthand that I would do anything for her because that's how much I loved her.

I place my head against the cool glass, calming me down after that frustrating phone call. I could pitch potential clients until I'm blue in the face, but I'm still Hartwell Berkeley's son. I'm the son of a man whose company was part of a scheme to bilk senior citizens out of their retirement savings. It doesn't matter that I had no knowledge of his crimes, nor was an active participant in them. People don't trust me.

Since being in business for five months, The DCB Group has a total of five clients and ten employees, including Eleanor, my assistant, who came over with me from Berkeley Holdings. It's a solid start, but I know if we don't find a client soon with the reputation that we need that would attract other potential income for us, my new company won't make it.

I sit back down at my desk and finger the silver Tiffany frame holding the photo of Allegra in Venice that also sat on my desk at my former company's headquarters.

I quickly pull out my cell phone and scroll down for the number.

Allegra's angelic voice fills my ear. "Hi, Harvard. Everything okay?"

"Yup. I just needed to hear your voice."

"That bad, huh?"

I sigh, leaning my head farther into the headrest of my chair, loving how she knows what I need from her just from one simple sentence. "Take my mind off it and tell me what you're up to."

I can sense her smile over the phone. "Nothing major. Lucy's here helping me rehearse and she's going to come with me tomorrow for my final dress fitting."

My heart warms at the thought of my Venus in her wedding gown. "Won't be long now, baby. Can't wait to see you in it."

"Or do you mean out of it?" she teases.

I can't help but smirk. "Usually, I'd say you were right, but there's nothing I'm looking forward to more than seeing you walking down that aisle to me, knowing that you'll officially become Mrs. Davison Berkeley."

Silence comes over the other end of the phone.

"Allegra, you still there?"

A quiet voice comes over the line. "Yes, Davison, I'm still here."

I close my eyes, smiling at the thought of her crying happy tears. "You crying?"

"No." She sniffles. "I'm fine."

I shake my head, laughing at her horrible acting. "Worst liar ever."

Her laugh carries over the phone. She knows I just busted her. And just like that, my Allegra is back. "Big-time. I'll see you tonight."

"I love you, Venus."

"Love you too, Harvard."

Chapter 3

Allegra

I will not look in the mirror... I will not look in the mirror.

"Darlin', you need to loosen up and smile. Why are you all serious? You're wearing the most beautiful dress I've ever seen in my life."

"Aww, bet you say that to all the brides, Mrs. Kelly."

"How many times have I told you to call me Maggie? And I swear on my beloved da's grave, love, this workmanship is just exquisite. Your ma must've looked like a film star on her wedding day."

"She did," I reply, thinking of the photo from my parents' wedding that's a permanent fixture on my father's nightstand, my mother smiling widely for the camera with Papa looking down at her so lovingly.

I'm standing on a small round raised platform in the tailor shop of Mrs. Maggie Kelly, the premier seamstress of the Upper East Side, as Davison's mother calls her. When Mrs. Berkeley found out that I was going to wear my mother's gown, she insisted that

I go to Maggie for the alterations. Mrs. Kelly is petite, a grand-mother of four and a native of County Galway, Ireland, with a strong brogue and a genius with a needle and thread.

I decided against a fancy wedding gown because I knew with-out hesitation that I was going to wear my mother's wedding dress when I got married. She had made it herself. Thanks to my Neapolitan grandmother who taught her how to sew, my mother was brilliant at it when she was alive. She made almost all of my clothes, and she knew where all of the best fabric shops were on the Lower East Side, just to the east of where we lived in Little Italy.

"I can't smile," I tell Maggie. "If I look in the mirror and smile, I'll start crying again because I can't believe it's really happening. After everything we've been through, Davison and I are finally getting married."

Maggie looks up at me from her kneeling position on the floor, a red pincushion wrapped around her left wrist. "You're marrying a lovely lad, Allegra. His ma is such a kind lady. One of my best clients. I'd do anything for her."

"I know. I couldn't have asked for a nicer mother-in-law. She was so helpful when I moved in with Davison, making sure I was fed and supervising the movers while I had a lunch break. God, that was an experience."

"What, dear? Moving?" she asks, her mouth full of pins. How she can talk with sharpened sticks of metal in her mouth, I'll never know. I suppose it comes with experience.

"Yes, but even more, incorporating my life with Davison's. It took some getting used to. He complained about the number of opera CDs I brought with me, while I had to demonstrate to him how to change the toilet paper roll in our bathroom."

Maggie shakes her head and murmurs, "Men," under her breath, and I share a laugh with her. "Hey, Lucy, how are the plans for the engagement party coming along?" I shout out to her.

"She's planning your engagement party? Lovely," Maggie remarks.

"I know. She didn't have to, but Davison sort of inadvertently mentioned it, and there's never a challenge Lucy will back away from. Right, sweetie?"

Suddenly, I hear someone sniffling and a tearing sound of something crinkly. I look over at Lucy, who is ripping open a bag of salt-and-vinegar potato chips, tears streaming down her cheeks.

"Lucy!"

"What?" she asks without looking up from her snack.

"What's going on?"

Her shoulders move up and down as tears run down her face. "Nothing."

My eyebrows furrow in curiosity. "You've come to every fitting with me, and you've never reacted like this before. Something's up with you."

She shakes her head. "It's nothing. I'm just happy for you."

I soften at my best friend's reply. "Thanks, sweetie. But I was asking you how the engagement party planning was going."

"Oh, fine," she mutters under her breath, her face buried again in the potato chips.

"Hey, if I didn't have Maggie sticking me with sharp pieces of thin metal, I'd come over and hug you."

"Too right, darlin'," Maggie agrees. "You'd look like a pin-the-tail-on-the-donkey game at a child's birthday party. Lucy, I've got a box of Kleenex on the side table there. Allegra, face forward."

I do as I'm told. "Yes, ma'am."

I take a deep breath and am about to allow myself to look in the mirror when I hear another tearing sound, this time something plastic.

I glance over at Lucy, and now she's pulling out a Twizzler from a jumbo-sized bag.

"Lucy! What the hell?"

She looks up at me, a red string of licorice hanging from her mouth. "What?" she mumbles.

"What do you mean 'what'? You're inhaling an entire package of salt-and-vinegar potato chips, and now you're digging into a feed bag of Twizzlers. What's going on with you?"

"I'm hungry," she murmurs, not even glancing at me, her focus fixed on the candy in her hands.

"Okay," I whisper, not convinced in the slightest.

"There," Maggie announces. "I think we're done."

Lucy joins me at my side when I finally look at myself in the mirror. I bite my lower lip to keep myself from losing it completely.

"You look beautiful, love," Maggie declares.

"Davison is going to lose his shit when he sees you, Alli," Lucy adds.

And now, at last, I allow myself to cry. I hear Maggie and Lucy start to sniffle as well.

I laugh to myself and shake my head at the sight of the two women, just to bring some levity to this moment.

"So, where are you going on your honeymoon?" Maggie asks. "Paris? Hawaii? Bora-Bora?"

"Nope, nowhere that exciting." I sigh resignedly. "Between Davison's new company and my rehearsal schedule, we're both too busy now. But Davison swears he's planning a special surprise for me."

She smiles at my reply. "Mmmm, that's lovely. Now give me your hand and I'll help you out of the gown."

"Oh, that's all right. Lucy can do that."

Maggie shakes her head. "Not on your life, darlin'. I'm not letting those sticky fingers covered with salt and vinegar touch this gorgeous gown. I'll have it pressed for you, and I'll call you when it's ready for pickup."

I take Maggie's hand and step down from the platform. "Oh, thank you. That would be great. Before I forget, could you give me the final bill? I brought my checkbook and—"

"No need. It's already taken care of," she informs me.

Lucy and I give each other puzzled looks, then I turn back to Maggie. "I don't understand."

Maggie grins at me, steps away to her desk, and returns with a letter in her hand addressed to me written in an elegant hand.

I slowly open the envelope with my thumb, careful not to rip it.

My dearest Allegra,

    I knew that if I told you I was doing this, you would protest and not allow me to give you this wedding present in return for the one you have given me—my son's happiness. I have never seen him so full of joy, finally being able to be his true self with someone who loves him for the man he is and not his name or money, and that is all because of you. You are so kind and sweet, and it has been such a pleasure to get to know the woman who will marry my only child, knowing that he has finally found the person he is meant to be with.

    Please allow me to do this for you. It is the least I can do for everything you have given to my son and me.

With love,
Mona

And that's when I completely lose it and start to cry, reaching for my phone to call Davison's mother. I take a deep breath, the phone shaking in my hands as his mother's voice comes over the line.

"Mom?" I whisper through my tears. I freeze, realizing what I just said. "I mean…Mrs. Berkeley…I mean…"

I can hear my future mother-in-law's voice start to choke up from the other end. "Oh, my darling girl, it's fine. You can call me 'Mom.' I'd like that very much."

I take a deep breath before I go on. "I just wanted to thank you for taking care of everything with Maggie. I read your letter, and everything you said…I don't even know where to begin."

"It's all right, Allegra," she replies in a soothing voice. "You just said it all. Why don't you come by for a cup of tea when you get home? We can talk more then."

I smile into the phone. "I'd like that very much. I'll see you soon…Mom."

"Good-bye, sweetheart," she replies before ending the call.

I press "end" on my phone and instantly dissolve into an ocean of tears. For a moment, I feel so guilty for calling Mona "Mom," thinking it's a betrayal to my own mother, *mia mamma*. But then, a flash of my mother's face crosses my mind, her shining brown eyes lit up in joy, her soft lips extended across her face in a wide grin. I think she'd be happy for me, that I found a second mom who will love me as much as she did.

Lucy takes me in her arms, embracing me tightly. "It's okay, Alli," she whispers. "I bet your mom is smiling down at you."

And this is why Luciana Gibbons, a blonde, smart-mouthed soprano from Tribeca with a big heart, is my best friend.

* * *

Once I use up Maggie's entire inventory of tissues, giving her a tight hug on the way out of her shop with Lucy, I pull Lucy aside on the street. The Maybach is idling on Madison Avenue as I watch Charles pop out to open the door for me.

"Charles, I just need a minute."

He nods and waits by the car. "Of course, Miss Orsini."

I turn back to Lucy. "Okay, talk to me, sweetie. What's wrong?"

She takes a deep breath. "Something's going on with Tomas."

"Like what?"

Her jaw clenches. "That's the thing. I don't know. He's been acting all sullen and moody. He won't talk to me. Every time I try to get him to open up, he says nothing is wrong."

I purse my lips. "I bet you it's nothing. It's probably just the pressure of being onstage, the demands he's under now. You know what that's like."

She sighs. "Yeah, I guess."

"Okay, topic two. What's with the snacking and the crying?"

Lucy's eyes glare back at me. "Give me a break, Alli. It's just hormones and PMS. Don't get your panties in a fucking twist."

I take a step back from her, completely caught off guard at her tone, which Lucy picks up on within seconds. "God, I'm sorry. I didn't mean to go all DEFCON 1 bitch on you."

I laugh, embracing her with one arm around her shoulder. "Hey, you're PMSing. You're allowed." I point to the Maybach. "Do you want a lift downtown?"

"No, no, I'll be fine. I might go for a walk in the park and just clear my head."

"Okay, but call me if you need to talk."

Lucy grabs me and hugs me good-bye. "I will. Promise."

I watch Lucy walk up the street and turn west toward Central Park.

Charles starts to open my door. I take two steps toward the car when I hear someone call out my name. It's a female voice, a voice I'd hoped I'd never have to hear again.

I spin around slowly. Standing before me is Ashton Canterbury, Davison's ex-girlfriend and the woman who took great pleasure in making my life a living hell. Yet she's not the same Ashton at all.

Instead of her typical ensemble of a sweater set, pearls around her neck, and headband holding back her blonde hair, she's wearing all black—a tight cowl-neck sweater, skinny jeans, and stiletto boots, and a quilted tote bag slung over her shoulder. Her hair is loose and flowing.

She is no longer the epitome of a WASP princess, but more like an editor from *Vogue*.

I turn back to look at Charles. "I'll be right back," I whisper.

He nods firmly in return. "Yes, Miss Orsini."

I walk away from the car as Charles shuts the door. When I look back, he is standing at attention against the car while watching me like a hawk.

I slowly approach Ashton, taking a deep breath before I speak. "Hello, Ashton. You look…"

She smiles stiffly. "You can say it. Different."

"Well, yes. If you don't mind me asking, what happened?"

"Let's just say I've met someone new." She looks up at the building. "You just came from Maggie's, didn't you?"

"Nothing gets past you, does it?"

"Rarely." She grimaces before opening her mouth again. "I suppose I should give you my congratulations."

"Not if it makes you physically ill."

She smirks at me. "I deserve that. Look, Allegra, I know we've had our differences in the past—"

I shake my head, laughing to myself. "Understatement of the damn year."

"But when I heard what happened to Davison, I felt terrible, and I was so grateful that he recovered."

I don't say anything, curious to see where this is going. I watch her face turn away from me, and when she looks at me again, her eyes are moist with emotion.

"Allegra, I'm not proud of what I did to you when you were dating Davison, how I sabotaged your performance at his mother's benefit. I'm ashamed of my behavior, and for that, I'm truly sorry."

I step back in complete shock, and quickly check the sky to see if any pigs are flying above me.

"I have to admit I never expected to hear that from you, but I appreciate that and I accept your apology."

She comes forward to me and touches my arm. "I truly do wish you and Davison all the best."

My natural instinct would usually be to pull away, as if her touch singes my skin. But her words and the tone in her voice make me think differently.

"Thank you, Ashton. I'll pass that on to Davison."

"Please do." She checks the rose-gold watch on her thin wrist. "I have to run. I'm glad I ran into you, Allegra."

"Same here," I reply, which surprises me when I say it because it's the truth.

Ashton gives me a quick smile and begins walking down Madison.

I shake my head in wonderment, heading back to the Maybach, where Charles is holding the door open for me once more.

"I guess miracles do happen, Charles."

He grins. "It would appear so, Miss Orsini."

Chapter 4

Davison

Leaning against the wall of my private elevator, I start tugging on my tie as if it were choking me. Another fucking frustrating day. All I need is Allegra and a tumbler of Glenlivet.

Fuck. She has rehearsal tonight.

The elevator opens to an empty apartment. I miss the nights when I would come home from the office and she would shout to me from wherever she was in our home—the bedroom, the kitchen, or sitting at the piano. Her voice alone can cure me of any stress or pain.

I turn for the bedroom, where I strip out of my suit and throw on my Harvard sweats, leaving my clothes on the floor, knowing Allegra will chew me out for it when she sees them there, but honestly, I love it when she does that because I'd rather hear her hurling her smart-ass admonishments at me than not have her with me at all, something that's happened more than I care to remember.

I walk into the kitchen, where I pour myself a Scotch and stare out into the living room. It's too quiet.

Drink in hand, I go back to the bedroom, put on a pair of sneakers, and grab my cell phone, keys, and wallet, heading for the elevator.

Two floors down, I step out and turn down the hallway to the corner apartment and ring the bell.

Dressed in a white cotton robe and a sky-blue silk pajama set with matching slippers, my mother, Mona Cabot Berkeley, opens the door.

"Davison, what a surprise," she greets me with a hug and peck on the cheek. She glances at the glass in my hand. "Tough day?"

I nod. "I'm sorry. Is this a bad time?"

She waves her hand dismissively at me. "Nonsense. Just come in already."

After the Feds seized my parents' home on Sutton Square for my father's crimes, I bought my mother a one-bedroom apartment in my building and told her she could decorate it any way she wished. She went with French country, a palette of soft yellow, rust red, and azure blue, a carved wood coffee table, and bookshelves and plush sofas you can sink into—much warmer than our former home with its stiff Regency furniture and antiques.

We ease down into one of the sectionals.

"Tell your mother all about it, darling," my mother insists, picking up a glass of white wine from the table and taking a sip.

I sigh. "I wish someone could tell me how long it'll take until people realize I am not my father."

"I hate to point out the obvious, but unless you change your name, I'm afraid that will never leave people's minds," she acutely observes. "Surely, you can't be doing that badly."

"No, we're not in horrible shape, but we could be doing much better. What could possibly have come over him when he decided to do what he did?"

My mother pauses before answering, slowly rubbing the stem of her glass with the pad of her index finger. "Hartwell was always obsessed with power and money. It didn't matter that his family was already wealthy. He wanted more, which in turn made him greedy."

I glance across at the photo on the mantel. I'm seven years old, posing with my father on a mountaintop in Gstaad, both of us outfitted in the finest skiwear, during one of our Christmas vacations when we still owned our chalet in Switzerland, until we had to turn it over to the authorities a few months ago as part of my father's penalty.

"I idolized him growing up, you know. I wanted to be exactly like him, always wanted to please him. I did what was expected of me, went to Exeter and Harvard. But it was all part of the image we had to maintain."

She nods her head. "Unfortunately, yes."

I watch as my mother absentmindedly rubs the base of her left ring finger.

"Still not used to it, are you, Mom?"

She looks down at the space where her wedding ring used to sit. "No, I'm not. It's just so natural for me, you know. It used to be such a comfort knowing it was there, but now it's like a ghost limb that's been cut off." She laughs and reaches for her wine. "You must think I sound like a complete loon."

"Not at all. Giving you a divorce was the most unselfish thing he's ever done. You know, I can't change my name, but you could always go back to being Mona Cabot."

She reaches for my hand, placing it over mine. "As long as your name is Berkeley, Davison, so is mine."

I clasp my fingers around hers. "Speaking of unselfish things, not that you've ever been selfish, but Allegra told me what you did for her with Maggie. That was incredibly generous of you, Mom."

My mom waves her hand dismissively in the air. "Oh, generous schmenerous. It's the least I could do. She was so sweet when she called me from Maggie's after she saw my note. That darling girl…" She shakes her head. "Whatever superior being decided to bring her into your life and mine, it was utter kismet. You're a different man now because of her. Knowing that my only child is happy means everything to me."

I smile as my phone *ping*s with an incoming text, then grin even wider.

Hey, Harvard, I'm home. Where the hell are you? I want to eat dinner with my fiancé.

My mother sighs. "Hmm. That smile only means one thing."

I lean over to kiss her on the cheek. "Sorry, Mom. Gotta go. My fiancée awaits."

We rise from the sofa together and hug each other tightly. "Give her my love."

"Will do. Love you, Mom."

"Love you too, son."

I swallow the last of my Scotch and sprint to the door, leaving the empty tumbler behind on my mother's coffee table.

* * *

The second the elevator opens, Allegra's voice fills the apartment. "Hey, Harvard! Do you want lasagna or manicotti? We still have some of Papa's leftovers and—"

Before she can say another word, I rush to the kitchen, taking in and admiring her state of clothing because all she's wearing is one of my Harvard shirts that falls to her midthigh. I pull her to me, slamming my mouth over hers. Within seconds, her tongue tangles with mine, her arms circling my shoulders to bring me into her as close as she can, her luscious tits pressed up against my chest.

When I pull my mouth away to hoist her up onto the counter, she pants, "Whatever you need, baby, just do it…I love you so fucking much."

She allows me this. My Venus. Her trust and her love are everything to me. Everything.

I stare into her eyes, seeing her love and hunger for me mirrored in them. She uses her hands to prop herself up so I can quickly remove her thong, dropping it to the floor, followed by her shirt.

"Spread, Allegra," I command her roughly.

She opens up her legs to me, and I dive for her pussy with my mouth. She is already drenched, and I devour her as if she were my last fucking meal on Earth, licking and sucking on her folds, then roughly pushing my fingers into her while laving her clit desperately with my tongue.

Her hands roam through my hair, fisting it tight, which only pushes me to the brink. Her muscles lock and she shudders in release, her warm essence spilling onto my tongue. I lick every single drop of it, savoring the taste of her in my mouth.

My dick is as hard as a fucking boulder. I need to be inside her now more than I need my next damn breath.

I yank her off the counter, then roughly turn her around to face away from me.

"I'm taking you from behind," I growl at her.

"Please, Davison," she begs in a husky voice, pushing her round, gorgeous ass toward me.

I take my cock in my hand, finding her sex, and smoothly slide myself into her. We moan simultaneously at the feel of us joined together. She is so hot and tight. Pure fucking bliss.

I grip her hips tightly and begin to thrust into her.

"Hard, baby," Allegra pants. "I need it hard."

She knows what I need. She knows me.

I start to pummel her. The only sounds in the apartment are our grunts and our flesh slapping against each other.

I won't stop until she comes for me. I want to hear my name on her lips when she climaxes because she is mine. I *need* to hear it.

Her sex clamps down on me like a damn vise. She is about to explode.

"Oh, fuck…Davison!" she shouts.

Her body shakes in release, sweat pouring down her back. My muscles lock, and I spurt into her over and over as I cry out in fucking ecstasy.

We stay still, panting hard until I catch my breath. I tug her to me, our sweat mixing together, my front to her back. Our legs are shaking. We can barely stand. She doesn't protest when I carefully ease out of her and pull her down with me to the floor.

Immediately, she wraps herself around me, our bodies now entwined.

She yawns. "Mmmm…I could probably fall asleep right here."

"Sounds good to me. I can't move."

"Same here." I can hear the smile in her voice without needing to see it on her face.

I run my hands through her silky hair as she places soft kisses on my collarbone.

"So, back to my original question, Harvard," she murmurs into my neck.

"Yeah?"

"Lasagna or manicotti?"

I laugh out loud, holding her tighter to me. I kiss her hair, bringing it to my nose and inhaling her coconut shampoo. I shut my eyes in silent thanks for this woman who loves me unconditionally. "Whatever you want, baby. Whatever you fucking want."

Chapter 5

Allegra

Eleven employees of Saxon Management, six men and five women, are sitting around a cherrywood conference table, all of them with their heads lowered as they check their cell phones. Drinking glasses and pitchers of water are placed in the center down the length of it. I'm at one end, with my manager Jared at my left. I stare at a black binder with the title STRATEGY SESSION FOR ALLEGRA ORSINI emblazoned across it.

"Let's get started, everyone," Jared announces to open the meeting. "First, I'd like to welcome our star of the moment, Allegra Orsini."

I smile and nod to acknowledge the light applause in the room.

"Please turn to the table of contents so we can review what will be discussed today."

I open the binder along with everyone else. The headings pop out at me, black ink bold against the white paper—DEBUT CD, ENDORSEMENT POSSIBILITIES, INTERNATIONAL RECITAL

TOUR. Then one particular section catches my eye—WARDROBE CHOICES FOR LA BOHÈME OPENING NIGHT.

Shivers run up and down my arms as I quickly flip to it. Jared's voice is white noise as pictures of various evening gowns look up at me from the binder.

I glare back at the page. "Excuse me," I whisper under my breath. Jared keeps talking.

"Excuse me," I repeat in a much stronger voice this time so I know I have his attention.

Jared finally pauses. "Yes, Allegra?"

I point down at the pictures. "This section with the dresses. What is it?"

My manager lets out a laugh, sounding as if he were caught off guard. "Look at you, clever girl, skipping ahead. We'll talk about it when we get there."

My blood starts to course hot throughout my body at the sound of condescension in his voice, clenching my hands together with my fingernails digging into my palms as I attempt to maintain some semblance of control. "No, I'd like to talk about it now."

A fake smile appears across Jared's lips. "Those are a few choices that your stylist is considering for you for opening night."

"I choose my own dresses, Jared," I inform him pointedly.

He laughs again, this time a bit more awkwardly. "Of course you do, Allegra. And you will choose one from a selection that our stylist finds. You're so lucky to have her on your team. Do you know who she's worked with in Hollywood?"

I purse my lips together, then take a deep breath. "I don't give a damn who she's worked with. I'll find a dress on my own. I know my taste. I have my favorite boutiques and vintage stores. I have a tailor who'll alter it if necessary."

A few snickers resound around the room, and I don't know if it's from the revelation that I shop at vintage stores or that I talked back to Jared.

Some woman speaks up, "Allegra, I totally understand what you're saying, I do. But we have to develop your brand as a team. Image is everything in this business."

I exhale and glance at Jared before I address the group. "Look, I truly appreciate what Jared and all of you are doing for me, and I'm grateful. This is just new for me, so there'll be a bit of a learning curve for me. Please understand that I'm slowly getting used to being back in the spotlight because of being with Davison. But I'm going to say this only once—I'm choosing my own damn dresses."

Silence falls over the room.

My knees start to shake under the table.

This isn't me. The dresses, the image. None of it.

"Allegra," Jared begins, this time a bit more stern, when the opening notes of "Nessun Dorma," one of Pavarotti's signature arias, fill the room. I reach into my purse for my ringing phone.

I swipe it open. "Papa, what's wrong?"

"I need to see you, *cara*. Can you come to the shop as soon as you can?"

At the sound of his voice shaking over the phone, I push back from the table. "I'll be right there."

I grab the binder and sling my purse over my shoulder. "I'm so sorry, but I have to go."

"Umm, Allegra, this is a meeting about you and your career," Jared practically growls at me.

I turn to him and look him directly in the eyes so there's no cause for misunderstanding.

"My father comes first, Jared. Always has, always will."

* * *

Charles pulls the Maybach over in the front of the apartment building on Mulberry Street in Little Italy, where I lived my entire life before I moved in with Davison.

I push through the door of the shop, where I'm confronted with two men in business suits, one of them measuring the counter with a retractable tape measure, the other making notes on his phone, and my father leaning against the far wall, his arms crossed and eyes glaring at the men with pure disgust.

I don't need to talk to Papa to know that whatever those two men are doing, it's not with his approval. "Excuse me! Who the hell are you and what do you think you're doing?" I shout at them.

The two men swivel their heads to me, both young, from the looks of them probably in their twenties in their ill-fitting suits that they probably bought to go on job interviews.

"And you are?" one of them dares to ask me.

Oh no, he did not *just say that to me.* "I'm Allegra Orsini, and this is my father's shop. So I will repeat myself: who the fuck are you?"

The tall, blond, blue-eyed one whose look totally screams "frat boy" straightens and looks me in the eye as his eyes roam over my body. "We work for the future owner of this building, Mr. Brett Pryce."

I dig my nails into my palms, doing the best I can to keep myself calm. I turn to my father. "What is he talking about, Papa?"

He steps forward to me, silently handing me a piece of paper. Some tacky logo is embossed at the top with Mr. Brett Pryce's name emblazoned in a gaudy font, with the body of the letter detailing his future purchase of the building, including the shop and Papa's apartment, the apartment where I grew up.

I've read enough. My right hand crunches the paper, its sound bouncing off the tiled walls of the shop.

I pivot back to the two assholes. "According to this, the purchase has not been completed."

Frat Boy smirks. "No, it hasn't. But it's just a matter of time until it happens."

I swallow in my throat to gird myself. This boy needs to be schooled, Italian-style. I walk up to the smart-ass, thrusting the crumpled letter into his chest. He rears back from the impact of my fist into his body, and I allow myself a quick triumphant smile. "Here's a news flash for you, Frat Boy. This piece of paper does not constitute a legal sale. Nobody needs to explain that to me, not even my fiancé, Davison Cabot Berkeley, the former president and CEO of Berkeley Holdings. Surely you know who he is."

"Yes, I do," he replies, his eyes locked on mine, but with his pursed lips and clenched jaw, I can tell I just unnerved him.

I take one more deep breath before I finish verbally wiping the floor with this prick. "Good, so I don't have to buy you a clue. Now I want you and your buddy over there to get the fuck out of my father's shop and if I see or hear that you've returned, I'm calling the local precinct because I've got them on speed dial, as does my father. The detectives there, they're my father's Saturday-night poker buddies, and they love Jimmy. That's what they call him, so if you dare step foot in here again, you'll be faced with a wall of blue the second you turn your back."

Frat Boy exhales, his eyes blazing fire at me. He pauses for a second, then growls, still glaring at me, "Scott, let's go," at the other guy.

The other guy brushes past us on the way out. Frat Boy gives me one more dirty, lascivious look. *That's it.* "I said get out, ass-hole," I hiss under my breath.

I stand perfectly still, daring him to say something else, but instead, he exhales deeply, his chest deflating in defeat, and walks out the door.

I hear steps behind me before the feel of my father's strong hands envelop my shoulders. "*Cara*, I don't play poker."

I smile. "I know that, but they didn't."

He kisses the back of my head. "My brave girl. So proud of you."

I twist back around to look at my father, his sweet eyes still worried. "You forget, Papa. Not only am I a New Yorker, but I'm also Italian. *Sono italiana.*"

He cups my chin in his right hand, the grimace now gone from his face, his eyes glowing with pride. I give him a quick peck on the cheek. "Come on, Papa. You need a drink. Let's go upstairs so you can tell me the whole story. *Andiamo.*"

I grab the crumpled letter from the floor and lead my father out, waiting for him to lock the door. Once we're upstairs in our kitchen, I grab the Sambuca, his favorite, from the liquor cabinet and pour us both a shot. I lean down and give him a quick kiss on the cheek, settling down into the chair next to him.

We clink glasses and quickly drink the bittersweet alcohol, wincing as it goes down.

Once we let the Sambuca warm our insides, I unfold the letter on the table. "Okay, Papa. According to this, the apartments are going to be made into co-ops. What about the shop?"

Papa sighs. "*Non lo so.* I really don't know. All of my customers are old or dead, none of their children or grandchildren live in the neighborhood, so I can't depend on their business. As much as I want to keep it, I don't see the point."

"But there is a point, Papa," I counter. "Your shop is an institution in this neighborhood. Everyone loves you. If they hear you're selling it, they'll be devastated."

"If I sold it, I'd have enough money to make the apartment co-op," he tells me reluctantly.

I take a deep breath. "I can talk to Davison. I know he would give you the money with no strings."

He picks up the glass and slams it back down on the table. "No! *Assolutamente non!* I will not take charity from anyone, most of all your fiancé!"

"Papa, I can tell you with absolute certainty that he could do it and he would without hesitation."

He takes my hand in his. "*Cara*, I know that he would because he is a good man. Believe me, I wouldn't approve of him marrying you if I thought he wasn't. But this is my life, my business, and I need to handle it my way."

I exhale. "Okay, Papa. But just think about it, okay?"

"*Sì*," he nods, patting my hand. "I will. Now, I have some leftover tiramisu in the fridge. Would you like some?"

I raise my eyebrows at him, giving him a look.

He laughs. "I know. Silly question."

I laugh in return and peck him on the cheek. "*Ti amo*, Papa."

He embraces me tightly. "*Ti amo anch'io, cara.*"

* * *

"I swear to God, if I see one circus acrobat or a mariachi band, I'm leaving," Davison informs me.

"I wouldn't be surprised, though. This is Lucy we're talking about. And this was your idea, big mouth," I remind him.

I can hear him hissing in reply as I laugh out loud at my fiancé's reaction.

Davison and I are holding hands as we ride up in the elevator of Lucy's apartment building in Tribeca. She lives with her parents in a loft, which they bought before Tribeca was known for its designer boutiques and trendy restaurants. The building was a warehouse back in the day, then it was converted into huge, cavernous lofts, with only seven residences in the entire building. Lucy's family lives on the top floor, with a beautiful roof garden and terrace.

No matter how many times I visit Lucy at home, I never know what to expect when I open the front door, and this time is no exception. Her father, Nigel, a tall Englishman, is an international dealer of modern art and well respected in his field, and usually when I walk in, his latest acquisition is sitting or hanging somewhere prominently in the foyer. And today, right in the center of the room, sits a stunning piece—a tall sculpture of a spider that fills up practically the entire space.

"Gorgeous," Davison remarks in awe. "I'm guessing it's a Louise Bourgeois."

"You'd be correct, young man," a posh British accent comments behind us.

Davison and I both look up and come face-to-face with Lucy's father, Nigel, tall and thin with salt-and-pepper hair, dressed casually but smartly in a pink button-down shirt, pressed blue jeans, and cocoa-brown suede loafers.

"Mr. Gibbons, it's so nice to see you again," I greet him as he leans in to kiss me on the cheek.

"Lovely to see you as well, Allegra. And I assume this is the young lad in question whom you've enraptured?"

Davison laughs. "Yes, sir. Completely. Davison Berkeley. It's a pleasure to meet you." He extends his hand to Lucy's father, who shakes Davison's hand firmly in return. "Looking around, I must say you have an impressive collection."

"Thank you. The pleasure is all mine," Mr. Gibbons replies. "Do you collect?"

"I have only a few pieces, a Rothko in particular that I'm fond of, but I'm always open to acquiring more."

"We should talk, then. Find me later," he tells Davison.

Davison nods his head. "Absolutely. I look forward to it."

"Well, then, let's get you to the party," Mr. Gibbons declares. "If my daughter knew I was keeping you, I'd never hear the bloody end of it."

He leads us farther into the loft, where the party is set up outside, with paper lanterns hanging from string hung all around the open space, and pink flowers in various forms, from peonies to roses, sitting in vases scattered all over the terrace. Round tables are set up covered in vintage linens, with a temporary bar standing to the side.

"About damn time!" Lucy shouts from across the terrace.

A DJ is set up in one corner, playing bossa nova music over the speakers.

"No opera music today, Alli, I promise," she says as she greets me with a hug.

"Brace yourself, Lucy. I actually don't mind opera music," I remind her.

"I know, but I thought a break would be nice, so it's going to be a nice mix of bossa nova tonight, maybe some classic eighties…"

"Joan Jett, perhaps?" Davison asks while simultaneously grinning at me wickedly, as if I needed to be reminded of the time I sang "Bad Reputation" to him on a karaoke machine while decked out all in leather, from the bustier to the boots with the six-inch heels, before he asked me to move in with him, sealing the moment with a marriage proposal, the best night of my life.

Lucy looks at him quizzically. "Yeah, I guess. I'm sure he has some of her songs. Look, go eat, drink, and enjoy yourselves. I have to go yell at the caterer now for forgetting to put out the miniquiches and bacon-wrapped scallops like I asked her to do fifteen minutes ago."

Davison and I watch Lucy walk away in a huff.

"Drink?" he offers.

"Like you need to ask."

As I watch Davison wander over to the bar, I don't see Papa or anyone else from my family, like Derek and Aaron or Davison's mother, but I do spot some former classmates from the conservatory, and I make my way over to them, embracing them and catching up with what's been going on in their lives.

A strong, warm hand suddenly lands on my shoulder. I turn and find Davison holding two glasses of champagne. "Thanks, baby," I tell him, taking one flute of the bubbly liquid from him, clinking glasses with him, then quickly making the necessary introductions.

"Would you mind terribly if I left you for a bit?" Davison asks. "Luciana's father is dying to show me his favorite pieces and talk some more."

I give him a short kiss on the lips. "Not at all. I'll find you later."

I break away from the group and find myself by the gift table. I had told Lucy that gifts were not necessary, but my best friend, being who she is, couldn't resist telling the guests that gifts were acceptable. Davison and I hadn't even planned on registering anywhere since we already had everything we needed when it came to the essentials, and honestly, it would've felt odd, a man of Davison's wealth asking our guests to buy him things like a toaster or a set of bath towels when he could purchase the entire registry himself.

"Congratulations, Allegra!"

I spin away from the table and smile when I see Lucy's mother,

Helena, in front of me. We give each other a tight hug. "I'm so happy for you," she says into my shoulder.

"Thank you, Mrs. Gibbons. Everything looks so nice."

Helena Gibbons is petite and curvy with gray eyes and light blonde hair, a spitting image of Lucy except for the blue eyes Lucy inherited from her father. Mrs. Gibbons is a former opera singer who gave up her career to stay at home with Lucy, which Lucy says her mother has never regretted.

"It's our pleasure. After everything that you and Davison have been through, you deserve this. We were more than happy to host the party."

"As if Lucy would've taken no for an answer," I add.

She nods at me. "Too right, my dear. I'd better go make sure she isn't driving the caterer crazy."

"Good idea."

I see waiters bringing out the quiches and the rest of the food that Lucy had mentioned, so she must've put the fear of Luciana Gibbons into the caterer. I head back inside to look for her just to make sure she wasn't losing her mind and to reassure her that everything was amazing.

I make a wrong turn in the loft, probably a bit light-headed from drinking champagne on an empty stomach, when I hear raised voices behind a closed door.

"What is wrong with you? You know Davison and Allegra. It's not like these guests are celebrities, for crying out loud!"

Oh fuck, it's Lucy shouting at someone. And my only guess who the person on the receiving end of that remark would be...

"Yes, but Davison is rich. Very rich. And so are you, Luciana," a low voice replies in a Czech accent.

Yup. Bingo. Tomas.

"For fuck's sake, I'm not rich. My father is. Can't you put aside your stupid aversion to people who have slightly more money than you, wipe that woe-is-me look off your face, and just enjoy the party?"

"I don't feel comfortable here," he mumbles.

"Well, suck it up," she snaps back at him, "because the party's just started and it won't be ending any time soon."

I hear a pause, and then, "I'll never be enough for you, Luciana," he says before yanking the door open.

I jump back in time before either he or Lucy can see me, hiding in the laundry room next door.

I poke my head out and see an empty hallway. Instead of looking for Lucy, I head farther into the loft, where I find Tomas staring at a Jasper Johns.

I quietly sidle up next to him. "Hey, Tomas."

He turns to me at the sound of my voice. "*Hallo*, Allegra." He stares at the painting, one of Johns's many representations of the American flag. "This is probably famous, yes?"

"It is. It's a Jasper Johns."

"And expensive probably."

"Very." I pause. "Do you know why I know who Jasper Johns is?"

"No," he replies with a grunt.

"Because Luciana told me. I had no real knowledge of art before I met her. I mean, sure, I knew who the *Mona Lisa* was, I could recognize Monet's lilies, but this modern stuff, I had no clue. The first time I came over here, I was so intimidated by everything. I was afraid to touch anything. But Lucy just laughed it off and told me who painted what and the meaning behind the piece, never once telling me what the art was worth because it didn't matter."

Tomas turns to me, his tall, strong body standing at least a whole foot above me as he looks down at me. "Allegra, my father is a farmer and my mother is a schoolteacher."

I shrug my shoulders. "So what? I'm the daughter of a butcher.

Do you think that matters to Davison? He doesn't care about the amount of money in my checking account. He loves me for me. And it's the same way Lucy feels about you. She doesn't care what your parents do for a living. She loves you for you. If you only knew how long she's had a crush on you."

He crosses his arms over his broad chest. "How long?"

I smile at the memory. "Since the day you first met when she bumped into you at school."

The sullen look on his face changes in a flash. "And then yelled at me for being in her way," he grins widely, recalling the moment just as vividly as me, probably even more so.

"You completely rattled her. She wasn't expecting someone like you on that first day of classes, but there you were, and she's been besotted ever since."

"Besotted?" he asks.

I smile back at him. "It means she was into you, Tomas. Big-time. She just never made a move because she was too afraid you'd reject her."

He shakes his head in exasperation, laughing to himself under his breath. "Stupid woman."

I nod in agreement. "Pretty much. She pretends to be all tough and strong, which she totally is, but deep down, she's just as scared as anyone else of falling in love with someone and finding out the other person doesn't feel the same way."

I watch as Tomas turns still, probably absorbing everything I've just told him.

I place my hand on his arm. "Look, just go talk to her. If you tell her what you just told me, I'll bet you she'll be much more understanding."

He nods. "All right. Thank you, Allegra." He leans in and pecks me on the cheek. "And congratulations."

I watch him walk away toward the kitchen when a pair of arms encircles my waist. "You okay, baby?" Davison whispers in my ear.

Without saying a word, I spin around in his embrace and kiss him on the lips, long, wet, and deep.

When we finally pull apart with only an inch or two between us, Davison holds me with one arm while stroking my cheek with the other. I can feel my eyes misting at his soft touch.

"What's wrong?" he asks me, more nervous this time.

I shake my head. "Nothing is wrong. Everything is fine. Someone just reminded me to be grateful for what I have."

"And that would be?"

I bite down on my lips to keep myself from crying. "Your love, Davison."

He takes my face between both of his hands and kisses me full on the lips. "Oh, baby, you always will," he whispers when he pulls his mouth from mine.

"Hey! Guests of honor! Get your butts outside! I'm about to give you a toast!"

Lucy's shouts cause Davison and me to pull apart, with Davison growling in protest under his breath. I turn and see Lucy standing with her hands on her hips, tapping her foot impatiently.

Davison swiftly twists me around back to him. "We'll be right there, Luciana," Davison shouts back to her, but with his eyes still locked on mine.

I hear Lucy stomp off. "It's not a good idea to piss off the hostess, Harvard," I inform him.

"I just needed one more minute, Venus."

"For what?"

He kisses me once more, softly and deeply. "For that."

Chapter 6

Davison

Charles is racing the Maybach north up the FDR Drive like a Formula One driver to take me to my final wedding tux fitting on the Upper East Side. I put down the copy of the *Wall Street Journal* that I'm reading and watch the various boats and barges sailing by on the East River. Ever since I've been with Allegra, she's taught me to look up from my laptop or phone once in a while and remember to appreciate the city I live in, even if it's just to admire the majestic skyline of our beloved city or see what's going on beyond the activities of the frenzied, insular business world that I work in. But at this moment, I'm actually thinking about the party yesterday and the moment I shared with Allegra in front of the Jasper Johns. And I know without a doubt that I'll never look at another Johns the same way again.

"Are you getting nervous about the wedding, sir?"

I look up toward Charles, who is staring at me in the rearview mirror.

I smile widely back at him. "Not at all. If it were up to me,

Allegra and I would have flown to Vegas and gotten married in one of those drive-thru chapels. But I wanted her to have the wedding of her dreams, so whatever she wants, she gets, with no complaints from me."

He laughs from his driver's seat. "I don't think Miss Orsini's father would have been too keen on you whisking away his only child to get married without allowing him the chance to walk her down the aisle."

I smile in agreement. "Indeed. I think he would've come after me with a meat cleaver and hunted me down to the ends of the earth if we had."

"She's a lovely young woman. And if I may say, the perfect match for you, Mr. Berkeley."

My heart softens at the kind words from the man who's been a father figure to me since I was a child. "Thank you, Charles. No argument there."

The Maybach comes to a stop. "Looks like there's an accident up ahead," he informs me.

I pick up the paper again. "No worries. We've got time to spare."

As I scan the pages, a headline catches my attention. "Like Father, Not Like Son: Heir to Swiss Pharmaceutical Fortune Looking to Branch Out." A picture of a young man accompanies the article right below the byline, a face I would recognize anywhere with his cocky grin and floppy hair.

I quickly reach for my phone and call my assistant. "Eleanor, I need to you get contact numbers for Christoph Kahn at Kahn Medical in Zurich, both business and personal…No, that's it. Just e-mail them to me ASAP once you have them…Thank you."

I end the call and stare out the window once more, grinning to myself.

In two days, I'm marrying the love of my life, and I may have just found the perfect client for my firm.

Life is fucking good.

* * *

Allegra

With my hand tightly in his, Davison leads me into Le Bistro, where we are about to have our rehearsal dinner and our wedding. This is the place that holds so many memories for us, the most important one of all being that this is where we first met when I worked here as a coat-check girl.

A cacophony of noise echoes down the narrow hallway from one of the private rooms in the back of the restaurant. Davison starts to walk in that direction when a realization comes over me. I tug on his hand, pulling him over to the side.

A worried look crosses Davison's face. "What's wrong, baby? Don't be nervous."

"It's been a crazy day, and I wanted to enjoy tonight without this hanging over me and you not knowing about it."

His hand grips me even harder. "You're scaring me, Allegra."

I swallow deeply and continue. "Do you know someone named Brett Pryce?"

He tilts his head in curiosity. "Yeah, by reputation. He's a sleazy real estate developer who takes great pleasure in violating every building code in New York City. Why?"

I sigh and inhale a deep breath. "I thought so. Papa called me very worried, asking me to come down to the shop right away, and when I got there, there were two guys measuring the shop for what's-his-name Pryce. He sent Papa a letter that he's buying his building, including the shop, and turning the apartments into co-ops. And you know Papa can't afford any of that. I'm so worried that—"

"I'll take care of it," he declares in that strong rumble of a voice that evokes the power and determination of a man who has the ability to make anything happen if he wishes it.

"I know, but, Davison, it's so much money, and—"

He takes my face in both of his hands, kissing me quickly but firmly. Then his eyes lock on mine, fierce and blazing in strength that sends electric pulses to every single nerve ending in my body. "It's done."

I know that it won't matter how long we'll be together, I will always be overwhelmed by the force of the unconditional love this man has for me and his unfailing generosity to anyone who needs it. I clamp my lips over his, kissing him long and deep. "Thank you, Davison" is all I can manage in a whisper when I pull away from him.

"Anything for you, baby." He kisses me fast on the lips. "Now let's go celebrate you becoming Mrs. Davison Cabot Berkeley."

I start to shiver in excitement. "Lead the way, Harvard."

We take the final steps together toward the space where our family and friends are waiting for us.

Entering the doorway, I take in the group gathered tonight. Everyone has drinks in their hands as servers make their rounds with trays of hors d'oeuvres. Lucy and Tomas are talking to Derek, our favorite accompanist from our alma mater, Gotham Conservatory, and Derek's husband, Aaron. Ian Parker is chatting with Davison's mother and Elias Crawford, the co-owner of Le Bistro and Davison's godfather, while Papa is in deep conversation with Signora Pavoni.

Lucy is the first one to spot us. "About damn time!" she shouts in her own loving way, and a loud round of cheers and applause rises from the group. Suddenly, Davison and I are separated as we're swallowed up by everyone greeting us at once.

It's only when the group parts slightly that I can take in the beauty of the room. I had decided on black and cream for the wedding décor, and I had shown Elias pictures I'd found on Pinterest of what I'd wanted the room to look like for the dinner. My breath is taken away because the reality is much more beautiful than I ever could have imagined. A long communal table stands in the center of the room covered in a cream tablecloth and linens. Down the middle of the table is a long black flower box with about a hundred cream roses standing upright as if they were sprouting from it. Small votive candles in petite black round glass candleholders line the outside edges of the flowers.

Lucy comes over to me, shoving a flute of champagne into my hands. "Here, drink."

She smiles at me, but her grin barely reaches her cheeks as she swirls a glass of clear liquid with ice in her right hand.

I frown at the sight of my best friend because I know without a doubt she isn't drinking water. Taking a sip of my drink, I pull her over to the side of the room. "Okay, what the hell, Lucy? You were all waterworks at Maggie's, and now you look like you'd rather be anywhere else than here."

She takes a huge swig of her drink. "Fucking Tomas. He still refuses to talk to me, and I've had it. Seriously, Alli, he's acting like such an ass, and I refuse to kiss it."

I glance over at Tomas, who is leaning against the wall, staring into his beer glass, a sullen look across his face just like the one he had in front of the Jasper Johns at Lucy's apartment.

I shake my head in exasperation, wondering why Tomas hasn't talked to her yet like he said he would, when I hear ice cubes clinking. I gesture to the glass in Lucy's hand. "What is that? Alcohol?"

"No, it's water. I'm feeling nauseous enough as it is."

I breathe a sigh of relief. "Oh good. I'm glad you're taking it easy."

Lucy glares back at me. "So what if it were? Who the fuck do you think you are? My sponsor?" she snaps at me.

My head rears back in shock, and I lean in closer to her. "Listen to me, whatever crawled up your ass tonight, shake it off, because this is an important night for Davison and me, and I'm hoping my best friend will show up eventually to support me."

She walks away in a huff and heads straight for the bar.

I shut my eyes in frustration, taking a deep breath to relax me.

A Southern accent snaps me back. "Drink up, darlin'; it's going to be a long night."

I smile as Derek and Aaron embrace me simultaneously. I kiss them both on the cheeks. "My favorite couple in the world. How are you?"

"Aaron is up for tenure at Columbia," Derek announces proudly about his husband, a history professor.

I give Aaron a celebratory hug. "That's wonderful. Congratulations!"

"Thank you." He thanks me in a quiet voice, always so modest.

Derek steps in closer. "May I touch the pretty?" he asks, pointing to a sleeve on my dusty-rose silk dress.

I smile as Aaron rolls his eyes and says, "Derek, really."

I laugh. "It's fine, Aaron. He did ask nicely, after all."

"That's because I'm a gentleman of New Orleans with impeccable manners," Derek counters. He swipes his hand over the fabric. "Gorgeous, darlin'. Love the shoes as well."

I lift one of my nude peep-toe patent leather pumps from the floor so he can get a better look.

He leans in for a closer look. "I approve."

"Well, thank goodness for that; otherwise I'd have to go home and change shoes."

Derek and Aaron smile at my reply when I see Lucy dash out of the room, nearly toppling Charles over in the doorway.

I quickly excuse myself and run after her. I look out into the hallway, but I don't see her. "Do you need me, Miss Orsini?" Charles asks.

"No, thank you, Charles. She's probably in the restroom."

I take off for the ladies' room, and when I open the door, I hear someone heaving in one of the stalls.

"Oh shit! Lucy!"

I rush to the paper towel dispenser and tug a few from it, soaking them under the water. I step into the stall and hold back Lucy's hair with one hand as she vomits into the toilet while I hold my breath to keep myself from retching.

She lifts her head and I shove the wet towels under her nose, watching as she takes them without a word. I listen as she moans, her arms moving as she wipes off her mouth. Then she shifts back and I offer my hand to help her to her feet.

When she finally turns to me, her face is pale, her light blue eyes bloodshot.

"Need water," she whispers.

I nod and get out of her way so she can get to the sink.

She cleans herself off more, swishing some water around in her mouth.

"Sweetie, what happened?"

Lucy stands upright, bracing the edge of the sink tightly with her hands. "Ugh," she moans. "It was probably the meat and dumplings I had with Tomas for lunch today. Maybe the meat was spoiled."

A thought rushes over me like a rogue wave. "Lucy, could you be…"

"What?" she asks as she wipes her mouth.

I shake my head. "Never mind. Ready to go back?"

"I'll meet you there. I want to fix my face."

"Okay, honey."

I head for the door when Lucy calls out, "Hey, Allegra."

I look back at my best friend. "Yeah, honey?"

"Thanks. Sorry I snapped at you before."

"When did you snap at me?" I give her a knowing wink and smile as I open the door. But the passing thought I had is now permanently etched in my mind.

* * *

After a sublime meal of a tomato-and-mozzarella salad, followed by lamb chops with fingerling potatoes and asparagus tips, pots of chocolate mousse are served with coffee and after-dinner drinks.

As I take a generous spoonful of dessert into my mouth, a hearty laugh rises above the voices of our assembled guests. When I look up, I see Lucy leaning over closer to Ian, who is sitting a seat away from her, the chair between them empty when Signora Pavoni left the room to answer a phone call. Ian is gesturing with his hands, and Lucy appears completely captivated by whatever he is telling her, smiling at him and touching him gently on the wrist.

Then I glance over at Tomas who's seated on the other side of Lucy, and his eyes are shooting fire at his girlfriend's back. With his entire body locked, I envision the dainty coffee cup in his right hand shattering into small pieces thanks to his tight grip.

Lucy doesn't even notice when Tomas throws his linen napkin on the table, rises from his seat, and storms out the door.

I push back and rush out to follow him. Just as I turn toward the main dining room to search for Tomas, a hand on my elbow pulls me the other way.

Davison starts to lead me down the hallway, his steps swift and determined.

"Davison, wait! I just—"

"I know."

"But Tomas—"

"I know."

We stop in front of Elias's office. He switches to his left hand to hold my elbow while he punches in the code to the keypad with his right hand.

Davison hauls me inside, locking the door behind us.

I turn to face him. "Why did you do that? I was going after Tomas. I don't know what the hell Lucy was doing, but he was clearly upset."

Davison shakes his head at me and laughs to himself. "Baby, I've watched you all night, and I love how much you always take care of others before you take care of yourself, like how you tended to Luciana when she got sick and how concerned you are about Tomas. But right now, you need to let it go and just be in the moment. Do you realize where you're standing?"

I glance around the room, and it hits me. We're in the office of Le Bistro, the room that holds so many memories for us. This is where I found out Davison would be serving as comanager to help Elias after he'd had a heart attack. Where Davison tended to me and let me rest on the leather couch after a customer harassed me. Where Davison kissed me when I wasn't sure about us, telling me how much he wanted to be with me.

Davison takes me into his arms, and I look into his eyes. "This is us," I whisper.

"It is. And the day after tomorrow, this is where you'll finally become Mrs. Davison Berkeley."

"Well, technically, our ceremony will be in the other room, not in this exact spot," I remind him.

He purses his lips together in amusement, takes a deep breath, then takes my face in his hands and kisses me so sweetly. "I can't wait to marry you, Venus."

"Likewise, Harvard. Now give me one last kiss in this office while I'm still Allegra Orsini."

He obliges without hesitation. Twice.

Chapter 7

Allegra

The fragrant scent of the apricot roses from my wedding bouquet permeates the interior of the Maybach. The florist who handled the arrangements for today tried to steer me toward lilies, but I was insistent on holding my favorite flowers when I walked down the aisle to Davison standing at the altar. I hold them up to my nose to inhale them again.

"They are beautiful, as are you, *cara*," Papa says, sitting to my right, holding my hand tightly. "I just wish Mamma could be here to see you in her wedding dress. *Bellissima*."

My eyes moisten at his words. I wipe them carefully with the ivory linen handkerchief that Davison's mother had slipped into my hands before she left the apartment.

"She is here, Papa," I assured him. "She always will be."

It had been such a chaotic morning, filled with much laughter and singing, thanks to Lucy belting out "Chapel of Love" on a damn loop. Both she and Mona helped me with my dress, hair, and makeup. Davison stayed over at his mother's while

Lucy took me out for sushi and beer for my last night as a single woman, staying over and sleeping in our guest room. Needless to say, this pleased Davison immensely due to the absence of a shirtless man slicked in oil shaking his junk in my face as he had worried would happen. We also decided to have the ceremony in the evening, with less chance of the paparazzi spotting us. As jaded as New Yorkers are, they tend to notice a woman in a wedding dress at lunchtime on Broadway and Sixty-fourth Street.

Lucy laughs from her seat up front with Charles.

"What's so funny?"

"Ian says Davison is pacing the floor like a robot vacuum out of control and is all anxious. He keeps saying to Ian, 'I just need to see her.'"

Something uncomfortable stirs inside me. I lean forward so I don't have to shout as loudly back to her. "Why is Ian texting you?"

"He's the best man, Alli. I'm the maid of honor. Enough said."

I bite down on my lip to keep me from yelling back, "No, that's actually *not* enough said!"

Why the hell…

No. Do not go there. This is not the time.

I shut my eyes and take a deep breath.

Davison is waiting for me. *He's pacing the floor for* me. *He needs to see* me. *He is about to marry* me.

Just as I open my eyes, the car comes to a stop in front of Le Bistro. The curtains in the front windows are drawn, as is the one on the door. Charles holds the door open for Papa, who in turn holds out his hand for me. Lucy sticks her head into the back to take the bouquet from me so I can make a graceful exit from the car.

I gather the hem of my dress and carefully slide along the seat, angling my legs out first so I can place my feet on the pavement as Papa's strong hand lifts me up. I duck my head so I don't mess up my hair from hitting my head on the car roof, because nothing is more attractive on a bride than a huge goose egg of a bruise protruding through her chignon.

Charles, Papa, and Lucy all huddle around me to shield me from any curious onlookers, moving me toward the door where Elias is standing, holding it open for us.

"He's waiting for you, Allegra. Whenever you're ready," Elias whispers, giving me a quick hug and kiss on the cheek before heading to the back room with Charles.

Lucy pulls out my makeup bag, which I shoved in her tote before we left. She hands me the compact as I check myself one last time.

"You look beautiful, sweetie," she says, giving me a final sweep with her eyes. "Now let's do this. Money Boy is waiting."

Thank God for Lucy. I allow myself to laugh to break the nerves and anxiety pooling in my stomach like a bubbling cauldron.

Lucy stashes her bag behind the bar and grabs her bouquet, slowly making her way to the back.

I pick up my bouquet and take a deep breath, looking at Papa. "*Andiamo*, Papa."

He smiles back at me. "*Andiamo, cara.*"

With my hand firmly in his, my father leads me to the back of Le Bistro, down the narrow hallway. Lucy stands in the doorway of the private room where Davison, the guests, the string quartet, and the judge are all waiting for us. She glances over at me, gives me a quick wink, then nods to the open door. I hear the opening notes of Pachelbel's "Canon in D" begin to waft softly from the room.

Lucy disappears into the room as my hands shake nervously. I take more deep breaths as I wait for it…

And then the quartet begins to play "Bridal Chorus" from Wagner's *Lohengrin*.

My cue.

Papa and I step to the entryway. I know everyone is looking at me, and I spot the flowers and candles placed around the room, but the only person I focus on is Davison, standing at the end of the aisle, wearing the tuxedo he bought specifically for today, classic black-tie, with an apricot rose pinned to his right lapel.

All he sees is me. Me in my mother's wedding gown—a long-sleeved lace dress with a bateau neckline and full A-line tulle skirt, with a silver vine headband accentuating my hair. He gives me a brief smile, but then his jaw clenches, and I know instantly it's because he's as overwhelmed with emotion as I am.

I don't even feel my feet on the aisle runner as Papa walks me down to Davison. I finally reach him, and he waits patiently as Papa gives me one last kiss, taking my hand from his and giving it to Davison's, ready and open for me. He shakes Davison's other hand and steps back to take his seat next to Mona.

I hand my bouquet to Lucy, holding on to the handkerchief. When I look into Davison's eyes, I see the moisture gathered in them. I gently dab his eyes, watching as he takes my hand to hold it to his lips to kiss it.

The judge clears his throat. "Not yet, young man." Davison and I allow ourselves a laugh for a touch of levity, as do our family and friends.

When we were planning the wedding, Davison and I decided to keep the ceremony simple. We didn't want something over-the-top. I was worried about Papa being upset that we didn't want a big church wedding so we could keep the wedding low-key and private, but he completely understood our concerns and said to do whatever worked best for us. After everything we've been through, we just wanted to be married. As we tightly hold hands and recite our vows to each other, my voice soft yet strong, Davison's practically booming, echoing throughout the small space, we officially commit ourselves to each other. He kisses my ring finger after he places my platinum diamond eternity band on it. Neither of us waits another second after the words "husband and wife" cross the judge's lips, when Davison cups my face and kisses me long and deep to whoops and applause. The quartet starts to play Beethoven's "Ode to Joy" as Davison and I kiss and kiss.

Davison's lips move to my ear. "Forever, Allegra."

"Forever, Davison," I whisper to him in return. Then we turn around to accept the hugs and congratulations from our friends and family.

* * *

In an adjoining room, champagne and hors d'oeuvres are passed around as Davison and I stand together, not leaving each other's sides for anything. He keeps rubbing my hand with his thumb, just like he did the first night we met.

I lean in closer to whisper into his ear. "So, Mr. Berkeley, could you give your wife one tiny hint where we'll be spending our wedding night?"

His warm breath caresses my neck when he whispers in return, "Patience, Mrs. Berkeley."

I groan in frustration.

"I look forward to hearing you do that repeatedly later tonight," he murmurs in reply.

The promise of that, the mere thought of it, causes me to turn wet with anticipation, and as much as I want to drag him into the office, lock the door behind us, and tear his new tuxedo off his hard body, I stay still and reply softly, "Bet on it, baby."

The gentle tinkling of cutlery against glass brings the ongoing conversations to a stop. My father is holding a spoon against his champagne flute. "If I could have everyone's attention before we sit down for dinner."

The room falls to a hush as Papa clears his voice. "For a very long time, it's just been my Allegra and me. I always wanted more for my daughter, and tonight, she has found her happiness. I know that Allegra and Davison are meant for each other because no matter what they've been through, their love was made even stronger as they faced those obstacles together. There is nothing a parent wants more for their child than to be happy, and Davison, my son-in-law, you have done that for my precious *cara*. *Grazie* and welcome to the family! To Davison and Allegra!"

"To Davison and Allegra!" everyone cheers in unison, raising their glasses to us.

Davison and I clink glasses together and we entwine our hands to sip from each other's glasses. "Cheesy!" Lucy shouts.

I untwist my hand, leaning into my husband. "Only a few more hours, Harvard."

"This is going to be the quickest meal I've ever eaten in my life," he promises.

Elias claps his hands together for attention. "Dinner is served, everyone."

Our guests begin to file out of the room into the hallway to the main dining room when Tomas captures me by the elbow.

"Allegra, I'm so sorry to bother you on such a happy evening."

I can see concern in his eyes. "What's wrong?" I turn to Davison. "Could you—"

Davison gives me a soft kiss on the lips. "No problem, Mrs. Berkeley. I need to check on something with my mother."

I smile widely, watching him walk away to Mona. I turn back to give Tomas my attention. "What is it?"

He exhales worriedly. "It is Lucy," he begins in his smooth Czech accent. "She is very friendly with this Ian. You are her best friend. Has she said anything to you?"

Oh God. I cannot get in the middle of this, at least not tonight, one hour after I just got married.

"To be perfectly honest, Tomas, she thinks you're pulling away from her. Have you spoken to her yet?"

He frowns. "No."

I sigh in exasperation. "Look, Tomas, the sooner you do, the sooner she'll stop being so friendly with Ian. I guarantee it. I think she's just looking for attention. The two of you just need to talk things out."

He pauses, then nods his head. "All right. I *vill* talk to her."

As he walks out the door, he looks back one last time into the room, his eyes narrowing, his face growing red in anger.

I shift my head to where he was looking. Lucy is standing with Ian, a huge grin on her face as they laugh and clink glasses.

Fuck. Lucy, what the hell are you doing?

A tug on my hand brings me back around. Davison pulls me into the hallway, pushing me up against the wall and taking my face in his hands. His hot mouth over mine, he kisses me with pure heat and passion. A low grunt escapes his throat.

"No more worrying about anyone else tonight," he pants when he releases me. "I know you love your friends, but for the rest of the night, you're not leaving my side. We're going to have our dinner, cut our cake, Ian will give his best man speech, you'll throw your bouquet to Lucy, then we're outta here. Deal?"

With Davison's heated eyes boring into mine, there is no way I'm going to deny him. "Deal, Harvard. Now let's go eat, because we're going to need our sustenance for tonight."

"Truer words have never been spoken, Venus."

Chapter 8

Davison

I hold my wife's hand in mine as Charles guides the Maybach through Saturday-night traffic. My tie is wrapped around Allegra's eyes so she can't see where we're going, even though I'm fairly certain she knows our final destination. Nothing gets past Allegra Orsini Berkeley.

"We haven't stopped yet for one traffic light," she remarks. "We're going home, down West Street, aren't we?"

"Maybe. Maybe not," I reply cryptically. "Maybe Charles is just hitting all the lights perfectly."

"Maybe," she mutters under her breath.

We turn right onto Battery Place from West Street, then onto Little West Street, where our apartment building is.

Allegra brings her hand up to her mouth, kissing my palm. "Thank you for bringing me home. Home is much better than any five-star hotel."

I soften at my wife's kindness, but I'm still intent on playing it out. "We're not home, Allegra," I insist.

I know without a doubt that she's rolling her eyes at me behind my tie. "Oh please, give me a little credit, Harvard."

The Maybach comes to a stop. I open my door and go around to Allegra's side, reaching in to help her out of the car, then picking her up in my arms.

Charles shuts the door once I've got a hold on Allegra. "Congratulations, sir. I'm so happy for you both."

"Thank you, Charles. And take tomorrow off, because God knows we won't be going anywhere."

He gives me a quick nod. "Thank you, sir. Good night, then."

"Good night, Charles, and thank you for everything," Allegra replies, extending one hand to him while holding on to me with the other.

Charles takes her hand and gallantly kisses it. "My pleasure, Mrs. Berkeley. Now, off with you two."

"You heard him, husband. Move it," my wife orders me as Charles laughs.

"Yes, wife," I obey her, giving Charles a quick nod, then making my way to the building entrance to our private elevator.

She smiles, and I know she senses we're going up in our elevator. "You can put me down now, Davison."

"Not a chance in hell. I'm carrying you over the threshold as per tradition."

"Can't argue with that."

The doors open, and I step through, my eyes widening at the view in front of me.

Allegra will love this.

"Not that I'm complaining, Mr. Berkeley, but since I know we're inside now, is there a reason you're not putting me down? Is something wrong?"

"Far from it, baby," I murmur.

I set Allegra down, positioning her to face the living room. "Keep your eyes closed until I say so. Okay?"

"Ordinarily, I'd say no—"

"Of course you would."

"But I'm too excited. I want the big reveal."

I undo my tie from around her eyes. "Then you shall have it. Keep them closed."

I walk around so I can see her face. "Okay. Open them, baby."

It was worth the wait. When Allegra sees the state of our home, her hand clamps over her mouth in shock.

"Oh, Davison," she whispers. "It's beautiful. When did you do this?"

"I didn't. Well, I did. I planned it, but Mom came over and took care of it."

It truly was more gorgeous than I imagined it. Tall ivory candles are lit all over the apartment, standing in various holders. The scent of apricot roses fills the room, huge bouquets of them positioned on the mantel and basically any flat surface. A bottle of champagne sits in a silver bucket on the coffee table.

"Shall we?" I ask my wife, holding out my hand to her. She places her hand in mine and I lead her to the living room. She waits patiently, watching me intently as I pop the cork and pour us the bubbly liquid.

I lift my glass to Allegra. "To my beautiful wife," I toast her.

"To my wonderful husband," she toasts in return.

We clink glasses and take a sip, then I circle my arm around her so we can sip from each other's glasses.

Allegra laughs. "Despite what Lucy said, this is definitely not cheesy, Harvard."

And that's why I love this woman.

"It's our wedding night. Cheesy is allowed, Venus," I declare.

She grins back at me wickedly, her left hand traveling over my chest, caressing my skin. "You look so hot, baby."

My cock hardens at the purr in her voice. "Do tell," I grunt back in reply.

"Mmm-hmm," she murmurs. "So, any other traditions you'd like to follow through on?"

"Just one," I reply, pulling her to me. I capture her mouth with mine, reveling in the taste of my wife. No longer able to restrain myself, I pull back and take our glasses, placing them on the coffee table, then lift her into my arms, carrying her hurriedly down the hallway to our bedroom, where more roses greet us.

I put Allegra down, giving her a quick kiss on the nose. "Why don't you get ready and I'll light the candles?"

I turn away from her, picking up the butane lighter my mom left behind to take care of the lighting in the room. When I finish, I look back and see Allegra still standing in the same spot, an incredulous look on her face.

"Baby, you okay?"

Her chin starts to quiver. "It's just…I can't believe we're here. I mean, I'm your wife, Davison. After everything, it finally happened, and I've never been so happy in my life."

At the sound of her shaky voice, my own mouth starts to tremble from the overwhelming emotion of this moment that I thought would never come.

I quickly stride over to her, taking her in my arms again and kissing her soundly. "I know. I feel the same way. We're home as Mr. and Mrs. Davison Berkeley. We did it. And I love you so much. So how about I help you out of this dress?"

She smiles through her tears. "I would like that very much."

I turn my wife around, reaching for the zipper at the top of her dress. I slowly lower it, revealing a white lacy ensemble underneath of a corset, garter belt, thong, and stockings. Then I release her hair from its chignon, allowing it to cascade down her back.

I spin her back to face me. She is a vision, the most beautiful thing I've ever seen in my life, and she is mine. All mine.

A lump catches in my throat. "You are so fucking beautiful, baby," I rasp. "I'm the luckiest bastard on the planet."

She pauses, then lifts up her index finger to my face, running it slowly across my lips, then across the top of her corset. My eyes travel along with her finger, my eager dick straining against the inside of my pants. "Then give me your masterful hands so I can get out of this thing, Harvard."

My insides start to heat from the intensity of this moment. I'm about to make love to my wife. "At your service, Mrs. Berkeley."

She turns around for me and I slowly unhook the clasps on her corset. Allegra emits a sigh of relief. "Oh, thank God. Now I can breathe."

I reach around her, grab her heavy breasts with my hands, and start to massage them. "How does that feel?"

Her head falls back onto my shoulder. "That feels even better, Mr. Berkeley," she exhales. She lifts her arms and coils them around my neck. "Mmmm, keep going."

I start to suck on her neck, then she curls her head so I can kiss her long, wet, and deep. When she pulls away, she twists back and looks me over. "Someone is wearing too many clothes."

Before I can say something, Allegra starts to unbutton the rest of my shirt and undoes my cuff links, dropping them to the floor. She cradles my sack in her hands, stroking it back and forth. I grit my teeth from the feel of her gentle hands on my cock.

"You keep doing that, and I won't make it to the bed," I manage through gritted teeth.

"Well, we wouldn't want that, would we?" she says, her voice low and deep.

My pants drop to the ground, and I step out of my shoes as she helps me with my socks. When she rises from the floor, she gives me a look with one of her eyebrows raised at me, quickly removes all of her exquisite lingerie, and jumps onto the bed. She leans back against the pillows and spreads her legs open, revealing her moistened pussy to me.

"Come here, husband," she beckons to me softly with a crooked finger, a look of pure lust in her eyes.

With the sight of her naked except for the stilettos adorning her feet, I can't hold back any longer.

"Get ready, baby," I growl, jumping onto the bed. I dive for her pussy, inhaling its musky scent, kissing her folds. Then I find her clit and suck on it hard. I clamp my arms around her upper thighs to hold her down as her body shakes and writhes.

"Yes, Davison," she moans. "Oh fuck yes, right there…keep going," she instructs me. And I obey my wife, now inserting my fingers into her waiting sex as she moves in tandem with my thrusts. I keep going. I'm going to pleasure my Venus until she is completely undone.

She bucks one more time, and her essence spills from her as I lick every last drop of it. Her legs collapse to the bed once I release them. I can hear her repeatedly panting, "Fuck!" as I crawl up her body.

I push her hair off her forehead as I stare into her dazed eyes. "Hello, wife."

"Hello, husband," she whispers back.

"You okay?"

She gives me a look as if to say, *Stupidest question ever*, and a huge grin.

"Good," I reply to her nonverbal answer, "because now I'm going to slide my cock into your wet pussy and fuck you hard and deep."

She closes her eyes in anticipation, inhaling deeply, her chest rising, presenting her beautiful tits to me. "Yes, Davison. Please."

It takes mere seconds for me to slide into her because she is more than ready for me. I fit inside her like a glove, perfectly, with no need for adjustment.

"Move. Oh God, please move," she begs.

I lean down and start to suck on one of her breasts while thrusting inside her. She moans as I bite her nipple, moving over to the other breast to give it equal attention.

Her hands run through my hair, fisting it, which only spurs me on. "Yes, baby. Faster, please."

I rise from her chest and take hold of her hands for balance as I start to pummel her, pounding my cock into her. The sounds of slapping flesh fill the room.

God, I fucking love that sound.

"Ankles around my waist. Now!" I command.

The backs of her shoes lock around me, the heels digging into my ass. I am impervious to the pain, too far gone in pure ecstasy to give a shit.

Our shouts and grunts echo throughout our bedroom. I work her harder and harder. "Yes, Davison! Yes! Yes!" she screams. Her muscles clench down on my cock as her body shudders and she comes all over me. Within seconds, I follow her into rapture, sheer fucking rapture as my cock releases inside her pussy.

Completely spent, I collapse onto her body, our sweat mixing together. Her arms immediately come around me, holding me as tightly as they can. Our breaths match as we both gasp for fresh oxygen.

I can feel her head twisting toward mine. "That was fucking amazing, Harvard," she pants into my ear.

I smile into her shoulder. "I aim to please, Venus. Once I've regained my strength, I'm going to get the rest of the champagne so we can replenish ourselves, then I plan on fucking you again."

"Mmmm, I would like that very much," she moans into my ear. "Davison?"

"Yes, baby?"

"Thank you for marrying me."

I turn my head and begin to suckle her neck. "Anytime," I murmur in reply as I feel her chest rise and body shake in soft laughter.

Chapter 9

Allegra

That's it, Allegra! Gorgeous! Now look into his eyes as if he were the love of your life."

The problem is I'm not looking at Davison. I'm standing in the arms of my costar, Luca Montes, who is the love of my life only onstage. Luca is happily married with a newborn daughter back in Spain.

I do as the photographer asks, and instantly, Luca and I burst into uncontrollable laughter. It's one thing when we're singing to each other about our undying love and he's begging me not to leave him. But in real life, Luca is a total cutup and can make me lose my train of thought with one roll of his eyes or mimic of a New York accent.

"Damn it, you guys! Will you keep your shit together?"

The crass admonishment comes from Jared, our mutual manager. We're doing a "Stars of Tomorrow" photo shoot for one of the opera industry trade magazines. I understand this kind of publicity is all part of the job, but what I don't get is why I'm dressed in a black leather strapless dress, stockings, and stilettos so high that Luca needs to hold me up, otherwise I'd be falling over straight onto my face. Meanwhile, he's decked out in a gorgeous black suit with no tie, his white shirt open at the top. Luca looks like he's ready for a night on the town, and my outfit reminds me of the time I dressed up for Davison as a wannabe Joan Jett and sang "Bad Reputation" to him, right before he proposed to me. Wrong music genre.

"*Lo siento mucho*, Allegra. So sorry. My back is starting to kill me."

"Your back? Try standing in these things for an hour. But thank you for the support."

"*De nada*. I just want to get home so I can Skype Pilar before she puts Amalia down for her nap."

"Of course. Okay, let's be serious now."

We shake our heads to get rid of the cobwebs. Luca places his hand on my face as if to caress my cheek as I stare deeply into his eyes. But without warning, he pinches my nose and emits a "Beep, beep!" before the photographer yells out, "I give up! Take five, everyone!"

Luca helps me over to a group of chairs on the side of the set so I can sit down and rest my feet. Then he collapses next to me, letting out a sigh of relief. Hair and makeup people rush over to us and immediately begin giving us touch-ups, with Luca and me trapped in a haze of hairspray.

I hear a set of heavy footsteps nearing us. "Do either of you have any idea how important this photo shoot is?" Jared yells at us.

Luca and I give each other a look. He sighs from exhaustion. "Jared, we've been doing this for more than an hour. And it can't be easy for Allegra in those shoes."

I tap Luca's hand with mine as a sign of gratitude. "More to the point," I add, "why am I dressed like I'm going to a sex club? Not that this look offends me or anything—I'm fine with it, but it has its time and place. I don't understand why I'm wearing something as dramatic as this for a magazine cover while Luca looks like he's about to hop into his Ferrari and cruise South Beach."

Jared's face is now turning fire engine red as he runs his hands through his hair. He steps closer to me, and I feel his breath on my face. "Don't give me this feminist bullshit now. If you're not ready to handle this level of publicity, then go back and sit at the kids' table until you're ready to join the grown-ups."

I start to shiver from the rage in Jared's tone. "I *am* ready," I reassure him. "I only wish I could just sing and not have to do all this."

"This comes with the package, Allegra," he reminds me. "If you don't want to be a star, then tell me right now so I'm not wasting any more of my time on you."

Suddenly, Luca jumps to his feet, planting a hand on Jared's chest. "That's enough. Just give us some space."

Our manager stares at Luca for a full minute before muttering, "Fine," and walking away, pulling his cell phone out of his pocket and scrolling it furiously.

Luca snaps his fingers and an assistant comes over, he whispers something in her ear, and she returns with a bottle of water with a straw. He takes the water from her and hands it to me. I smile at his kindness. "Thanks."

"So you won't ruin your lipstick," he points out.

I playfully nudge his elbow with mine. "You're the best, Luca."

He stares at me, but not in a leering way. "You remind me of Pilar. Same fire: you're not afraid of anything..." he says wistfully.

I frown at his obvious sadness with his family so far away. "Are they coming over for opening night?"

A huge smile stretches across his face. "*Sí*. I can't wait to show them around New York."

I take a long sip of water, but before I can get it to go down, an overwhelming need to cough takes over my entire body, and I can't stop. The water escapes my mouth and drips down the front of the black leather dress. My throat feels raw, like someone scraped the inside of it.

Luca jumps to his feet, shouting, "We need some help here." Suddenly, a mob of people surrounds me, assistants and stylists barking instructions at each other, someone wiping down my dress, Jared yelling, "What the fuck is going on?" And the entire time, I'm doubled over, my hand over my mouth, trying to cover my coughs, desperately wishing for them to stop.

"Give her some space!" Luca orders everyone, his one arm holding me by the shoulders, and I can see the other extended toward everyone, with his hand facing palm out to keep everyone at bay.

When I think the coughing has finally dissipated, I pull myself up, staring into a sea of eyes, some with concern in them, others impatience, Jared's being the latter.

"What the hell, Allegra? Did you take up smoking or something?"

I glare back at him as Luca helps me sit down. I wipe my mouth with the back of my hand before I reply. "I don't know where that came from, Jared. I'm fine. But thank you for your concern."

"We've been rehearsing nonstop, or did you forget about how stressful that can be for a singer?" Luca adds. I can see the fire in his eyes aimed back at our manager. His left hand rubs my right shoulder, reassuring me that he's got my back.

"What about the dress?" Jared shouts at the photographer. "Can you still work with it?"

Luca and I look at each other, shaking our heads at the complete lack of compassion from our manager.

The photographer steps closer to me, narrowing his eyes as he studies the front of my dress. "It looks fine. It's a good thing this is black. But we can always fix any mistakes with a little airbrushing. No need to worry."

"Good. Then let's finish this already," Jared yells, as if he's directing this shoot.

One of the assistants hurries over to me with a mug, and I see steam rising from it. "Hot water and lemon. I hope this will help."

I want to hug this girl. "Thank you so much."

She nods and just as quickly scurries away. Jared comes over to me again, but before he can say something, Luca holds his hand up to him again. "Five minutes. Just give her five minutes."

Jared mutters something unintelligible under his breath before walking away.

I put my nose to the cup in my hands, letting the steam permeate my nose as I take deep breaths of it. Then I take a slow sip of the hot liquid, mentally noting to make sure that I thank that assistant once more before I leave, because this is exactly what I needed.

Luca rubs my back soothingly. "Better?"

I sip the hot water again before answering. "Much."

His body shifts closer to me. "Allegra, are you sure you're well?"

I nod. "I think so. But that scared the crap out of me."

"And me. Do you think you need to see a doctor?"

I shake my head. "No. Like you said, I think it's just everything. The rehearsals, the pressure, all of this," I reply, waving my hand at the wide expanse of the photo studio, everyone focused, rushing about doing their jobs.

"But you would tell me if something was wrong, *sí*?"

"Of course. And thank you for saying all that before to Jared, by the way. I could've handled myself with him. You didn't need to step in."

He shakes his head amusedly. "Just like Pilar. I know, but it's not right when a man speaks to a woman like that. I get very protective."

I grin. "And you remind me of Davison."

Luca slaps his hand against his forehead. "*Ay!* I completely forgot! *Felicitaciones!* How was the wedding?"

"It was lovely, thank you. Everything was perfect. We'll have to have you and your family to our place for dinner when they come over."

"*Gracias.* We would enjoy that very much."

The photographer shouts again for everyone to get back into place. Luca stands up and holds out both hands to me to help me to my feet.

"Allegra, I know it's been a long day for you. But the sooner we get this done, the sooner we can go home. And I promise not to make you laugh."

I nod my head. "Let's do this."

My costar leads me to the backdrop, and he once again places his hand on my face as I stare into his eyes, pretending he's the only man for me.

* * *

I walk into my father's butcher shop, the familiar smell of freshly sliced meat making me hungry within seconds. The customers greet me with hugs and kisses.

Papa works his way to me through the crowd. "*Dio mio!* Such trouble I have to go through just to hug my own daughter!"

I embrace my father, then let him lead me around the counter to the back room. We sit down on the crates lining the walls, like I used to do when I was little, watching Papa and Mamma work out front.

"Espresso, *cara*?" he asks, pointing to the coffeemaker on the counter.

"No, Papa. I'm good."

He reaches out to my face, touching it with the tip of his index finger, then checking it when it comes up covered in makeup. "What is all this? You don't go out like this, do you? You're beautiful just as you are."

I smile at Papa, ever the parent offering positive reinforcement at a moment's notice. "No. I just had to do a magazine photo shoot with Luca. I came straight here and didn't have time to wash it off."

"Do you want to go upstairs to clean up?"

I shake my head. "I'll do it when I get home. I just wanted to see you. It was a long morning. This whole thing, my career, the constant publicity, it's difficult to get used to, since that's not how you raised me."

"And with good reason. I did it to keep you safe."

I nod in agreement. "I know. And I'll always be grateful for that. But this is my life now, and I just have to learn to deal with it, because this is what I've dreamed for as long as I can remember."

"I can't wait to see you up there. I just wish…"

"Mamma," I whisper. "*Lo so*. I wish that too."

I reach down to get a tissue from my purse when I spot an open newspaper lying on a crate near me. I pick it up and see it's open to real estate listings, with a few circled in Queens. "What's this?"

"What does it look like? I'm looking for a place to live after I sell the shop."

I throw the paper down in frustration. "Papa, I told you that

Davison is more than willing to help you out. I've already told him about it, and it's as good as done. And the guy who wants to buy the place, what's his name…Brett Pryce. Davison said he's a total creep."

"No, Allegra! I told you I won't take any money from him. It's a matter of pride."

"Ha! It's a matter of you being a stubborn horse's ass!" I counter.

He shakes his head vigorously, jumping from his seat and now pacing the floor, muttering all sorts of things in Italian.

With his back to me, I hear him take a deep breath. "It's very nice of your husband to offer." He pauses. "Fine. I'll listen to what he has to say, but I'll still say no."

I grin to myself, pursing my lips together when he turns around so he can't see how happy I am now. I stand up to give him a tight hug. "*Grazie*, Papa."

I pick up my purse and begin to walk out when Papa pulls me back by the elbow. "*Aspetta, cara!* You're not going anywhere without taking home some food to feed that man of yours."

I sigh in exasperation. "I do cook, you know. So does Davison, believe it or not."

He waves his hand at me dismissively. "Eh! That's fine, but there's nothing like the best Italian prosciutto thinly sliced with a side of melon. At least I can give you that."

Papa grabs an apron from a hook on the wall and holds it out to me. "You can do the honors. How do you say, I'm 'keeping it true'?"

I laugh out loud. "Keeping it real."

"*Sì*, keeping it real. You may be a future star on the stage of the Met, but here on Mulberry Street, you're still Giacomo Orsini's daughter, who works the counter at her father's butcher shop."

I take the apron from him and give him a quick peck on the cheek. "*Sempre*, Papa."

Chapter 10

Davison

With my suitcase lying open on the bed, I begin to fill it, traveling back and forth to the closet with more clothes to pack in it. The moment I've been dreading since the wedding two weeks ago has arrived. Tomorrow, I leave for Switzerland to meet with Christoph Kahn, my childhood friend who I contacted to pitch him the services of DCB Group after I read that article about him in the *Wall Street Journal*. He was still the same Christoph I remembered from our school holidays in Europe—cocky, outgoing, and smart. We agreed to meet after the wedding, and now that the time has arrived, it's killing me.

I return from the closet carrying several pairs of socks, drop them into my suitcase, then stop to stare at my wife. Allegra is lying in bed dressed only in my Harvard sweatshirt, going over the notes her *La Bohème* director gave her after rehearsal tonight, then picking up the sheet music and quietly alternating between humming and singing as practice.

This image of Allegra, this is what I look forward to seeing for the rest of my life.

Between my work and her rehearsals, we didn't have time for a proper honeymoon, so we made sure to play hermit on the weekends, never leaving our apartment, ordering in, and fucking each other until our bodies were fully sated.

I go back for my underwear, finding my socks gone from my suitcase when I throw it in.

"Baby?"

She doesn't look up from her notes. "Yeah?"

"Where'd my socks go?"

"How should I know? You're the one who's packing."

I raise my eyebrow at her. "Okay," I reply, now completely suspicious.

I grab a bunch of ties, and now my briefs have disappeared from my case.

"Allegra!"

"What?" she asks, again only focusing on the papers in front of her.

I'm about to ask her again when I notice the bedsheets around her have become bulkier, increased in height. I pull the linens back, revealing my socks and my underwear, her notes flying up into the air.

"Venus…" I sigh.

She frowns at me and gives me a shrug. "Can I help it if I don't want you to go?"

I haul the suitcase from the bed, place it on the floor, then join my wife on our bed, pulling her into my arms. "I know. I don't want to go either. But you know I have to. This is business."

She sighs. "I know. I'm usually not a selfish person—"

"Very true," I quickly agree with my wife.

"—and I would never ask you to put me before your business."

I shake my head. "Allegra, you will *always* come first. I hope you know that by now."

"Of course. You're building your business, and getting this Christoph guy to sign on with you would be a huge coup for you. It's just we've been together every night—"

"Except the night before we got married, which I still think was unnecessary."

She rolls her eyes at me. "It's called tradition, Harvard. But getting back to my point, I know your career is important to you, as mine is to me. I just miss our quiet nights at home, watching a movie on the sofa, cooking together, spending lazy mornings in bed."

I kiss Allegra's hair as I hold her tighter. "And we'll do all that again really soon, baby, once we get our professional lives in some kind of order. We'll find our balance. You know that, right?"

She nods. "I do. I just...Tomorrow morning is going to kill me, saying good-bye to you."

I quickly disentangle myself from my wife, hurling the unpacked briefs and socks over my shoulder. "Then let's say good-bye now properly."

Allegra's eyes light up in recognition, and she mirrors my actions, pushing all of her papers to the floor, followed by ridding herself of the sweatshirt, revealing her lush, succulent tits, which instantly make my dick rock-hard at the sight of them.

She pulls my face to hers, plunging her tongue into my mouth. "I think I'm going to like your version of good-bye," she pants when she comes up for air.

I roam my hands over her, pinching her nipples. "I aim to please, Mrs. Berkeley."

Her hands lock their grip on my face so her eyes can bore into mine. "You always do, Mr. Berkeley. Now fuck me hard."

I dip my head to her chest, murmuring under my breath as I devour her left breast, "Always, baby. Always."

* * *

With its stark white walls, dark trim, and turreted towers at each end, the Gstaad Palace hotel sits atop a tall hill in the Swiss Alps, hovering over the small village, serving as a beacon at night when illuminated from the outside. I'm in my suite waiting for Christoph Kahn to arrive, coffee and tea at the ready. We agreed to meet here instead of Zurich, where his family's company is based, to take the pressure off the meeting and keep it more casual since we haven't seen each other in years.

From my balcony, I can see the chalet that once belonged to my family, where I spent so many vacations as a child. After my arrival late yesterday, I had my driver take me past it so I could see it. The last time I was there was to help my mother clear out our belongings under the watchful eyes of the local authorities so we wouldn't take anything deemed valuable that could be seized by the Feds as outlined in the agreement between them and my father's lawyer.

When the car drove up to the house, signs were posted to the front door and the garage door, all in German, declaring the house had been seized and warning against trespassers. It broke my heart. I had hoped that one day I could bring Allegra here for vacation, to watch our children open their presents here on Christmas morning, after which we'd spend a full day on the slopes. But that would never happen, and I vowed to myself that I would find a new home for Allegra and our family where we would spend our holidays so we could make our own memories.

A knock at the door snaps me out of my reverie. I stride over to it, open it, and standing in front of me is Christoph, wearing a cream turtleneck sweater, pressed blue jeans, and black soccer shoes.

"I think one of us is overdressed, man," he smirks, staring at me in my charcoal suit.

I grin back at him. "One of us never grew up, I see."

We shake hands, slapping each other on the back. "Good to see you, my friend," he says in greeting. "Been way too long."

"I know. Have a seat. Coffee?" I offer.

He slouches down onto the couch. "Yeah, thanks. Black. Had a long night last night."

I pour the coffee and hand it to him. "And her name was?"

"Brigitta and Elsa. You can meet them tonight if you like."

I shake my head, raising my left hand to him so he can see my wedding ring. "Sorry. I'm officially off the market as of a few weeks ago."

He takes a long sip of coffee. "Pity. Could've been like old times."

I sit down on the other sofa opposite him. "We did have some crazy nights, I'll admit. But Allegra is it for me. Never been happier in my life."

Christoph visibly winces. "I'm allergic to marriage, man. But I'm pleased for you."

"Thank you. So, about the piece I read in the *Journal*..." I begin.

"Yeah, my father wasn't too happy about that. He prefers to keep our affairs out of the public eye."

I sigh, worrying that this meeting might not go the way I'd like. I open my laptop, clicking on the PowerPoint presentation I made for him. I turn it around to face him. "Look, I know that I've been in the news thanks to my own father, so I made this for you to reassure you that—"

He waves his hand in the air at me. "Don't bother. I know you're not your father. God knows I've had so many issues with my own father, which is why I can't do the corporate thing anymore. It's too much stress, but I do love business. What I need is someone to tell me where to put my money."

"And I can do that for you," I tell him, my voice strong and unwavering.

He smiles at me, leaning back into the sofa cushions, stretching his arms out across the back. "Why do you think I'm here? I don't get up before noon for anybody, but you're Davison fucking Berkeley, man. I saw what you did with your family's company before all that shit went down. You're a genius with money. Harvard doesn't give out MBAs to morons."

As encouraged as I am by what he just said, I hesitate before I ask my question. "So, are you interested?"

Christoph leans across the coffee table, holding out his hand to me. "Fuck interested. We have a deal. Just send me the contract."

My eyes pop out in surprise as my shoulders sink from the relief, taking his hand to shake it in return. "You can trust me, Christoph."

He laughs out loud. "My friend, after all the shit we pulled as teenagers and all the times you covered for me with my parents, there's nobody I trust more with my money. All I ask is that if I find a potential investment, you come see it for yourself, no matter where it is—Hong Kong, Dubai, wherever. And our next meeting will probably be in Zurich in two weeks."

I mentally calculate the timing. Allegra's opening night at the Met is in two weeks. I quickly steel myself, so that Christoph can't read the worry on my face that there might be a possible conflict. "Of course. Whatever you need. You're my client. Comes with the territory."

"Excellent." He checks his Rolex. "I'm starving. Any chance you could have lunch with me?"

"I'd love to, but I promised Allegra I'd get home as soon as I was done here."

"You couldn't spare an hour? I've already got some ideas in mind. Surely you don't have a flight to catch, since you probably have your own jet."

I take a deep breath. *He's right. And he just agreed to sign with me. Allegra will understand. This is business.*

"Of course I do. Lunch would be great. How about that pub where we always went for burgers to get our hangover cures?"

Christoph points his finger at me excitedly. "*Ja!* Great idea, man. Let's go."

I get up from the sofa. "Just give me a sec. There's no way I'm wearing this suit to a pub, especially *the* pub where we once got kicked out after we got in a fight with those royal snots."

"Those were the days, my friend." He slaps me on the shoulder. "This will be good. I can feel it."

Finally, I can breathe easier. "Thanks, Christoph. I think so too."

Chapter 11

Allegra

"You WHAT???"

Davison takes a deep breath, then looks at me straight in the eyes. "I have to meet with Christoph in Zurich the week of your opening night at the Met."

I can't believe this. We've just had his welcome-home dinner, which I ordered in from his favorite Chinese place around the corner, preceded by my jumping into his arms the second he stepped out of the elevator into the apartment and assaulting his lush mouth with mine. I was hurrying with putting the dinner dishes away into the dishwasher so I could get ready for sexy time with my husband when he laid this news on me.

I put down the dirty plate back into the sink, turn to him, and hold up my wet hands, palms facing out, before I go on. "Let me get this straight. The week that I'm making my debut on the stage of the Metropolitan Opera, something I've dreamed of since I knew I wanted to be an opera singer, that's the week you decide to fly to Switzerland on business?"

"I didn't choose that week, Allegra. Christoph did. And I have to do as my client wishes."

"But didn't you tell him you couldn't?" I ask.

"No, because—"

My mouth drops in shock. "What do you mean 'no,' Davison? Did it just slip your mind? Am I that fucking forgettable?"

If there's such a thing as green fire, I can see it in my husband's eyes, which are ablaze with it at this moment. "Fuck no, Allegra!" he shouts in my face. "Christ, don't you *ever* think of yourself that way with me! I didn't tell him because I'll be home with plenty of time before that. It's just one meeting. One overnight stay, tops. And I didn't tell him because I know it won't be a problem. I mean, you won't need me until the day of, right? And what happened to being so understanding about my work?"

He's got me there.

I exhale, taking a dishcloth to wipe off my hands, then turn back to face him. "Okay, you're totally right about that. I did say that. But you have to understand, Davison. I'm nervous as hell already about that week. The final rehearsals, the last fittings. It's all going to be too much, and I just need to know that you'll be home. This is something that's going to come up again and again when I'm performing. Hopefully, one day, I'll be making my debut in London at Covent Garden or in Milan at La Scala, and I'll need you to support me. I'm freaking out that something will happen, and I want to know that when I come home after a long night, whether it's here or at a hotel, you'll be waiting for me."

"I won't be."

My chin starts to tremble and I'm about to burst into tears. "What?"

"I won't be home or in our hotel room because I'll be in the audience watching you, silly woman."

I gasp from relief and pull my husband to me as I dissolve into tears. "I'm so sorry, Davison. I'm such a wreck. I didn't mean any of it."

I can hear the smile in his voice. "I know, baby," he coos in my ear. "I just have to remember that artists can be a bit sensitive."

"Just a bit." I laugh. "And you business types aren't exactly known for being mushy or in tune with other people's feelings, because all you care about are dollar signs."

Davison suddenly pulls away from me, but still holds me by the shoulders, a puzzled look on his face. "Umm, did we just inadvertently insult each other?"

I clamp one hand over my mouth. "Oh shit! I think we did. But I wasn't hurt because it's true. I am a sensitive opera singer who needs constant reassurance and positive reinforcement."

"And I really am a heartless businessman and all I care about is money and the bottom line," he adds.

We pause to look at each other and collapse into peals of laughter. Davison takes me into his arms once more and envelops my face firmly between his hands. "You know what else, baby?"

"What?"

"We just had our first fight as husband and wife."

I pull back in surprise. "You're right." I stop for a second, then realize I need to say something else. "I'm sorry, Davison. I know you'll be there. I shouldn't have doubted you."

"I'm sorry too. I just need to be more understanding when it comes to you and what being a professional singer actually entails."

"Apology accepted. Now that we've made up, we still need to do one more thing."

"Which is?"

"Make-up sex!" I shout, rushing out of the kitchen down the hallway to our bedroom, Davison's feet thundering on the floor right behind me.

*　*　*

The stage lights of the Metropolitan Opera warm my face, my makeup adding a second layer of skin that I cannot touch for fear of smearing it. The orchestra follows the guiding baton of our masterful conductor as the audience sits in rapt attention.

Luca is holding me to his chest. The sweat from his face touches my cheek, the heat from his body enveloping mine. I am lifeless in his arms, my eyes now closed and arms hanging at my sides as he sings mournfully, calling out Mimi's name in grief, with me as Mimi finally succumbing to tuberculosis.

But my exterior appearance is polar opposite to what is happening inside me. My heart is pounding inside my chest. My debut performance on the stage of the Metropolitan Opera is coming to a close. There were no slipups, and my voice did not waver once. I sang with strength and passion, as did our entire cast. Blood is rushing like a geyser through every vein in my body, the excitement of this night heightening my nerve endings and adrenaline coursing out my ears. My dream has just come true.

The curtain falls to the stage as the thunderous applause from the packed house takes on a life of its own, full of emotion and appreciation. Luca whispers in my ear, "We did it, Allegra!" as we kiss each other on the cheek. We rush off, following the rest of the cast to the stage floor to take our curtain calls. From behind the curtain, I step out with Luca and the main players as shouts of "Bravo!" echo throughout the Met. Then we step back behind, allowing the supporting players to take their bows. I follow again with Luca, our director, and our conductor who has joined us from the orchestra pit. Luca then steps out with me for our mutual curtain call, then Luca takes his solo bow, and finally, it is my turn.

I walk out to the crowd, and the crowd erupts with calls of "Brava! Brava!" The director comes out and presents me with a huge bouquet of red roses. I kiss him on both cheeks, then gesture to the orchestra with my hand over my heart as a sign of gratitude. Finally, I look up into the Berkeley family private box to see Davison and my loved ones. I see Papa, Lucy, Tomas, Davison's mother, and Signora Pavoni.

My heart drops. Davison is not there.

I plaster a smile on my face and bow one last time, then wait as I watch Luca and the rest of the cast come out for a final curtain call.

I walk with the cast backstage to our dressing rooms so we can change into our evening wear for the opening night afterparty on the Grand Tier balcony overlooking the plaza of Lincoln Center. My dresser, Gwen, who's worked at the Met for twenty years, helps me remove my costume, wig, and body microphone.

"You were lovely, dear," she congratulates me. "I'll just go return these. Be right back."

I nod silently to her as I slump down into my makeup chair. Tears threaten to take over me. There must be a reason why Davison wasn't there.

I reach for my purse and rummage for my cell phone. When I power it on, a flurry of *ping*s sound off, followed by texts from Davison.

Thunderstorm in Zurich. Airport issued a ground stop. Will keep you posted.

Finally got the all clear. I'm on my way, baby.

Nightmare traffic on the Turnpike. GWB backed up. Charles is doing his best.

Finally on the West Side Highway. Be there ASAP. Love you, Venus!

I sigh in disappointment. He called me yesterday to tell me that Christoph asked him to stay one more day, so he couldn't exactly say no. But now it doesn't matter. He may as well have stayed another week.

He missed it. He missed my debut, my opening night at the Met.

Before he left for Zurich to meet with Christoph, I told him again that I wasn't angry at him for going because this was business. We made up after the fight, having make-up sex more than once because we just weren't sure that once would be enough; it was our first fight, after all.

Hmm, do you feel like we've made up enough? he asked.

Mmmm, I don't think so. I think we should do that again—you know, just to make it official.

I lost count after four, of how many times it took to make it official.

But I understand that his work is important to him. And I have no right to be angry now, because he can't control the weather.

I walk to the en suite bathroom and hop into the tiny shower, scrubbing the makeup off with my face wash and a hand towel, refreshing me enough to let me put on a brave face for the partygoers and well-wishers so my disappointment over Davison's absence doesn't show.

I put on a slinky silver gown that I found at a boutique in SoHo for the party. It's not something I would normally wear, with its plunging neckline and tight skirt, but Lucy said it looked perfect on me, and insisted I get it because how many times do I have a debut at the Met?

I blow-dry my hair, reapply my makeup, then slip into a matching pair of silver stilettos. I give myself a once-over in the mirror, checking to make sure my poker face is intact.

I shove my wallet, phone, compact, and lipstick into my clutch, and make my way through the backstage area to the elevators to take me to the party.

When the doors open, the noise from the party assaults my ears. I show my ticket to the guard, who gives me a smile as he takes it from me. Suddenly, I'm surrounded by the cast, Jared and his team, and so many other people who I don't know.

Luca appears from nowhere, shoving a flute of champagne into my hand. "Drink, Allegra. We deserve it."

"My savior. Thank you." I give him a smile and take a sip of the bubbly liquid.

A tall, willowy woman with sleek black hair stands next to him. She smiles at me, extending her hand. "Allegra, it is so nice to finally meet you. I'm Pilar Montes."

I take her hand and shake it warmly. "I'm glad I can finally put a face to the name that Luca talks about nonstop," I tell her.

They both look at each other, sharing a loving grin. "Is your husband here?" Luca asks. "I'd love to meet him."

"No," I reply with a forced smile. "He got stuck in bad weather in Zurich, but supposedly he's on his way. I know we'd love to have you over for dinner one night, maybe after the run is over."

Pilar nods. "We would enjoy that very much."

I see Lucy elbowing her way over to me, with Tomas, Papa, and the rest of my family close behind.

"Would you excuse me? I see my family about to pounce on me."

"Certainly. I'll see you tomorrow," Luca replies before taking Pilar's hand as they head for the bar.

Lucy finally reaches me, grabbing me in a tight hug. "Alli! You were so amazing!"

I hold her tightly, trying to keep my emotions in check because in all honesty, it's Davison I'd rather be hugging. "Thanks, sweetie!"

Everyone takes their turns congratulating me, but Papa hangs back. When he finally steps up to me, he holds me and whispers, "You were so lovely, *cara*. But I know you. You're sad because Davison wasn't here."

"*Sì*, Papa," I murmur into my father's shoulder. "Did he tell you about the storm?"

"He called his mother. She wasn't pleased."

I pull back from him, shaking my head. "Oh no. But it was the weather. It wasn't his fault."

"Doesn't matter. She's his mother. She has the right to be angry at her son."

My father's face begins to turn red. I sigh. "Oh God, now you're mad at him too? *Per favore*, Papa, give him a break. He's trying to build his business. I understand that."

"But you're my daughter, and—"

My eyebrows rise in curiosity when Papa stops talking without warning and focuses on something happening behind me. He nods and grunts. "*Bene*."

I turn around. Everyone's eyes are on me as Davison walks toward me determinedly, his strong jaw clenched and his emerald eyes locked on mine, with an enormous bouquet of apricot roses in his hands.

I freeze in place, waiting for him to come to me.

He finally reaches me. "Allegra," his voice rumbles in that way that always arouses me to my core. I take the roses from him and wrap my arms around him as I start to cry uncontrollably. He lifts me from the floor, claiming my mouth with his as everyone around us cheers and applauds, watching my husband kiss me with pure, uninhibited ardor.

After we kiss for what seems like ages, he breaks away from my lips, his warm breath tickling my ear. "Do you need to schmooze with anyone else? I can wait, but just barely."

"Don't worry, Harvard," I reply, trying to catch my breath. "Just need to say hi to the board of trustees."

As I hold my roses in one hand, Davison pulls me by the other to the group of well-dressed women and gentlemen gathered in one end of the room. He knows them all, of course, and they greet him warmly. Watching him charm the women and talk finance with the men, I'm aroused from simply being so close to him, enraptured by the sheer power of confidence he exudes. It is pure male, and I need him inside me, that power overwhelming me, pushing me to the edge until I can't think and I am desperate for release.

I don't even realize how entranced I am by him until I hear him ask me, "Ready?"

I can barely nod in reply before he hauls me out of the room. I try to acknowledge my friends and colleagues on our way out, but he's eating up the carpet with every step.

"I need to get my things from my dressing room," I pant as we head for the elevators.

"Lead the way, baby. Quickly," he growls back at me.

We finally reach the backstage area, and I unlock my dressing room. Davison slams the door behind me and pushes me against it. My roses drop to the floor as I tug my husband to me, devouring his mouth, hooking one leg around his waist. His hands roam over my body, reaching my breasts as he kneads them through the thin silver fabric.

Coming up for air, Davison starts rambling, "Baby, I'm so sorry. God, I was so desperate to get to you and the weather wouldn't let up, then the fucking traffic on the Turnpike, and—"

I stop his mouth with my index finger. "It's okay, Davison. I know you did everything you could to get here. I was devastated when I didn't see you in the box during the curtain call, but once I saw your texts, I felt better. And there will be other performances."

He runs his fingers over my cheeks, staring at me as if for the first time. "What did I ever do to deserve you?"

I melt at the look in his eyes, closing mine at his soft touch. "I think we both finally deserved some happiness in our lives."

"Mmmm, I agree," he moans. "I can't believe how understanding you are about all this. I wish my mom could've seen it your way. She read me the riot act when I called her about my plane being delayed."

"Yeah, my father wasn't too pleased with you either," I inform him.

His head falls back as he sighs. "That's just great. Even my father-in-law is pissed at me."

I bring his head back up so I can look him in the eyes. "Hey, Harvard, you know that rush you get after Harvard beats Yale at anything, even rugby?"

"Harvard doesn't have a men's rugby team," he states matter-of-factly.

I shake my head. "Whatever. You know that feeling I'm talking about, right?"

He nods his head vigorously. "Hell yeah. Nothing like it."

"Well, I've got that same adrenaline rush going now, Davison. You understand what that means, right?"

His emerald eyes blaze up in comprehension. "Get your shit, baby. We're taking the long way home with stoplights, because there's no way we're waiting until I get home to fuck my wife long and hard."

I push him away from me so I can get to my tote bag on my chair. I shove my clutch into it, along with my makeup and water bottle. I sling the bag over my shoulder, tugging Davison's hand as I shut off the light.

"Let's go, Harvard."

"Fuck, I love it when you're bossy, Mrs. Berkeley."

* * *

Davison

I can't believe I'm doing this again. It's three days later. My suitcase is at the elevator, Charles is downstairs waiting to take me to Teterboro, and Allegra is in my arms as we say good-bye to each other.

"This is killing me," I declare, gritting my teeth. "I mean, Christ, I just saw Christoph how many days ago?"

"Davison, remember why you're doing this. It's business," Allegra reminds me.

"I know, but your second performance is tonight, and I promised—"

"And again, husband of mine, there will be others, so stop whining and go. At least London is a bit closer this time."

"Only by, like, an hour, flyingwise. Frankly, I'm a little hurt that you're so eager for me to go." I laugh.

Allegra smiles, but I can already tell it's forced because it doesn't extend across her entire face.

I bring her closer to me. "What's wrong, baby? I was just joking."

"It's just…"

I raise her chin with the tip of my index finger. "Tell me."

"I know how important your work is to you. I just don't want…"

"Go on."

She exhales a long breath before continuing. "I'm scared you'll become like your father: obsessed with money and power. That I won't recognize you anymore."

Her admission shakes me to my core. She saw what my father's crimes did to my mother and me. I can't blame her for feeling like this.

Her face is fixed on the floor. "Allegra, look at me."

Finally, her dark brown eyes rise to meet mine. "Baby, as long as I have you to ground me, I will never become my father. And you're not planning on going anywhere, right?"

A small smile escapes her lips as she shakes her head. "Nope. You're stuck with me, Mr. Berkeley."

"Good, then it's settled. You have to stay with me to keep me from becoming a megalomaniacal Master of the Universe. Deal?"

My wife leans into me. "Deal, Harvard," she whispers before her lush lips cover mine as she dives into my mouth with her tongue.

We kiss and kiss until we sense it's time to let go. "You'd better go, baby," she insists, albeit reluctantly.

I pull away from her, picking up my laptop bag. "Back before you know it." I hug her tightly one last time. "I love you so much."

"I love you too. Now go do your thing."

I kiss her quickly before I roll the suitcase to the elevator and press the call button. The heavy doors open. I step in, turning back to my wife one last time.

"Forever, Allegra," I call out to her.

"Forever, Davison," she replies, a glorious smile stretching across her beautiful face.

Chapter 12

Allegra

Luca Montes has a beautiful voice. I'm not at all surprised about the glowing reviews he received for our opening night. I'm listening to him now singing as Rodolfo in Act I, exchanging jokes in his Paris garret with his friends Marcello, Colline, Schaunard, and Benoit. Everyone except Rodolfo walks off the set through the garret door, pausing as they sing the lines Puccini wrote with an offstage direction.

Now it is my turn. I wait for the assistant stage manager's cue, then sing my first line behind the door. I take a deep breath, waiting for Luca to open the door for me, holding Mimi's unlit candle and key to her room. I swallow quickly in my throat and pivot my head from side to side. For some reason, my neck has been killing me since the party, but I think nothing of it. Gwen also made me some hot water with lemon as she was dressing me because she didn't like the sound of my voice. I just brushed it off, telling her I partied too much on opening night.

Luca and I ease into the scene, as we have from the first time we rehearsed it, smooth as silk. I could not have asked for a more dedicated, giving acting partner than him.

As he finishes singing about Mimi's freezing hands, I inhale deeply, then launch into my aria, "Sì, mi chiamano Mimì," the lyrics of which I know as well as the Lord's Prayer by now. The words, the notes, the meaning behind the aria, they are as vital a part of me now as my own flesh and blood.

Luca and I wait a few moments as we always do after I finish because, inevitably, the audience will applaud me for the opera's signature aria. We smile at each other, then Rodolfo's friends sing to him, beckoning him from the courtyard to join them at the café.

Finally, Rodolfo sings of his love for Mimi, and I sing in reply, reciprocating the emotion that she feels for him in return.

Luca leans in to kiss me, which we have down to a professional science with the perfect angle for our heads and mouths.

I pull away, about to object to his kiss. But when I open my mouth, nothing comes out. My voice…it's…It's just gone. I try one more time, tears forming in my eyes from frustration and helplessness. Luca's eyes pop open in panic, and he quickly blinks them and gives me a short nod to tell me he knows something is wrong. He is remembering what happened at the photo shoot. He is right here with me, ready to protect me as his costar and friend.

I quickly regain my senses and glance over to Julia, the woman who is working as the prompter for tonight's performance. She sits in a box at the edge of the stage at the level of our feet. Her job is to give cues and pitch when necessary, but right now, with one look from me, she knows she needs to sing my lines as I mouth them in sync with her.

Thankfully, we only have a few lines left before the act is over. Luca grips me tightly, and I know he is still in the scene as

Rodolfo, but in reality, right now he is Luca, my singing partner and good friend who is as worried as I am about what's just happened to me.

We exit the garret in character, then I listen as Luca and Julia sing the last two lines together, despite the fact that she is out front and we are standing offstage.

Within seconds, the Met stagehands are changing the set for Act II, the square in Paris with its shops and café where Rodolfo takes Mimi to meet his friends. There are hundreds of extras, including animals to corral, which requires a five-minute pause to set up between acts.

Our assistant stage manager, Peter, comes running over, fear etched across his face. "Allegra, what the hell happened?"

When I open my mouth, I begin to cough. I cover my mouth, and when I pull it away, my palm is covered in my blood.

Suddenly, Peter shouts into his headset, ordering my understudy, Gina, to the set and for someone to text the doctor on call. Luca yells for a tissue before he hands me off to Peter, kissing my hair and telling me he'll see me as soon as he finishes tonight. I simply nod as the cacophony around me turns into white noise, and then the ground below my feet disappears.

* * *

Davison

I bound up the front stairs of the New York Eye and Ear Infirmary of Mount Sinai, taking two at a time. I push the glass doors open, rushing for the reception desk.

"Where is urgent care?" I demand breathlessly.

The woman points to her left. "Around that corner, sir."

I run in the direction she indicated, pushing through another set of doors, targeting the check-in desk as soon as I spot it.

"Where is my wife?" I pant to the nurse on duty.

"What is her name, sir?"

"Allegra Orsini Berkeley."

She checks her clipboard. "She's in exam room two. I can show you—"

I don't bother to wait for directions. I need to see Allegra right now. Right fucking now. I rush down the hallway to a set of rooms, scanning the signs outside for the right one. My shoulders sag in relief when I see it, barreling through the door, not giving a fuck who's inside, if I've got the wrong room, any of that shit.

But I have the correct room, because Allegra is lying on a bed in a standard mint-green hospital gown.

"Baby!" I growl, rushing to her, desperate to hold her in my arms.

She sits up at the sound of my voice, tears streaming down her face. Her entire body is convulsing from her sobbing, as her arms shoot out to me, eager for my touch.

Within seconds, I'm holding her. "I'm here, Allegra. I'm here. Tell me what happened."

Her arms encircle my waist like a vise, with her hands fisting my jacket. She won't stop shaking.

With one hand, I smooth her hair back. "Please, baby. Talk to me."

But she doesn't say anything. She only whimpers like a wounded, defenseless animal.

"She can't talk, Davison."

Her father's calm voice gives me a start. I turn to see him slumped in a chair in the corner behind me. "Shit! I mean...Mr. Orsini, I'm so sorry...I didn't see you there."

He rises to his feet and slowly makes his way over to me. "*Per favore*, don't apologize. I'm just glad you finally made it."

I hold Allegra's shoulders with one arm while holding her hand with the other. "I was already on the ground at Teterboro when her manager called me to tell me she'd collapsed backstage, then that she was taken here after she was first examined at St. Luke's over by Lincoln Center. What happened?"

Mr. Orsini's eyes are sunken, his face fallen as he begins to explain. "Apparently, she lost her voice during the first act, then when she came offstage, she started to cough up blood. The ambulance took her to St. Luke's first, but when the ER doctors said it was her throat, Jared insisted she be brought here because the Eye and Ear Infirmary also has a voice subspecialty—that's what he called it."

I nod. "They do. I Googled it in the car on the way here. So she can't speak at all?"

A tug on my jacket brings my attention back to my wife. She grunts something, pointing at herself, as if to say, *Hello! I'm right here! Talk to me!*

I caress her soft cheek. "I'm so sorry, baby. Of course. Have you been examined yet? Are you waiting for test results?"

She nods vigorously.

"Do you have to stay overnight?"

She shrugs her shoulders.

"Fine, then we'll wait to find out, but if you do, then I'm staying with you. Did Jared leave?"

"Yes," her father replies for her. "He said he'll be in touch in the morning."

A tall woman in a white doctor's coat with a light brown ponytail and round tortoiseshell glasses walks into the room, carrying a manila file. "Hello, Mrs. Berkeley. I'm Dr. Laura Bauer, the resident on call. From what your tests indicate, your vocal cords have sustained some damage, and I want you to stay overnight so we can monitor you, and then in the morning, the chief voice specialist will study your films and results and can consult with you then. Is that clear? Do you need anything?"

Allegra shakes her head, then points to me. Dr. Bauer smiles. "I take it that's your husband. So you have everything you need?"

Touched by my wife's sweet nature, I kiss the top of her head as she nods and gives the doctor a thumbs-up.

"Very well, then. We'll have you moved into a private room shortly. I'll see you in the morning. And remember...no talking."

Allegra nods. "Thank you, Doctor," I reply in thanks for both of us as we watch the doctor leave.

Her father steps closer to the bed, taking Allegra's other hand. "*Cara*, do you need anything before I go?"

She shakes her head, then points to herself, her heart, and finally, Papa.

His eyes tear at his daughter's gestures. "*Ti amo anch'io.* Call me in the morning when you know something, okay?" He says that to Allegra, but I know it's really meant for me.

"Of course we will," I assure him.

Mr. Orsini gives his daughter one last hug, he shakes my hand, then leaves the room. Allegra begins to pat down my jacket, then my ass.

"Baby, as much as I'd love to, I don't think this is the time—"

She rolls her eyes at me and smacks me on the arm. Gesturing with her hand held up to her ear, she acts out talking on the phone, and then the realization hits me.

I pull out my phone, which she grabs from me and immediately opens to the notepad app, typing furiously.

Phone in purse. Left behind in dressing room. Nurse never showed up with paper and a pen.

I nod in understanding. "Allegra, tell me what happened."

More typing.

Lost voice during first act. Prompter sang for me and I mouthed the words. Came offstage and coughed up blood.

Oh my God. I hold her tighter as she continues.

Then I fainted and woke up in ambulance with Jared next to me. He was in the audience and someone rushed out to get him. You know the rest.

She pauses and looks up at me, then types some more. *Don't leave me. Scared.*

I take my wife's face in my hands. "I'm not leaving you for a second. If you have to spend the night here, then so am I."

She starts to cry again. I take her in my arms, soothing her as I run one hand over her hair again and again. "It'll be okay, Allegra. Whatever happens, we're in this together. Why don't you lie down?"

I release her and let her fall back onto the bed. She moves over to the edge of the mattress, patting the empty space next to her.

Right now, I don't give a shit if Nurse Ratched comes in and yells at me for violating hospital rules. If my wife wants me next to her, nobody is going to stop me.

I kick off my shoes and carefully slide onto the bed, wrapping myself around her.

"I'm here, Venus. I'm here," I whisper to Allegra, watching in relief as her eyes flutter closed for some much-needed sleep.

Chapter 13

Allegra

From the north-facing windows of the office belonging to the chief specialist for voice and throat at the New York Eye and Ear Infirmary on Second Avenue, I can see the tall spire of the Chrysler Building on Forty-second Street, and the Citigroup Center only a few blocks farther up.

In two separate chairs facing the doctor's desk, Davison is sitting next to me in one of them holding my hand. He's freshly showered and dressed after a quick trip back to the apartment before our appointment. Thankfully, I'm now in a sweater and jeans that he brought back for me instead of that scratchy hospital gown.

"Columbia," he mutters.

I pull out my phone and start to type on it: *What?*

He looks down at his phone, and with a derogatory snort, he points to the degrees on the wall. "Princeton undergrad, and Columbia Medical."

I slap him on the arm. *Unbelievable. I swear, this doctor had better have good news to give me, because not being able to talk back to my husband when he's being a total ass is beyond frustrating.*

I quickly type, *Give it a rest, Harvard. I can practically see the ivy growing on the damn walls, so zip it! Got it? Where he went to medical school should be the least of your worries right now.*

He shuts his eyes, takes a deep breath, then lifts my hand to his lips and kisses my palm. "I'm so sorry, baby. I'm just nervous."

I restrain myself from typing out, *Join the fucking club.*

Finally, the door opens behind us, and an older man of medium height with salt-and-pepper hair comes around to shake our hands. "Mrs. Berkeley, Mr. Berkeley, I'm pleased to meet you. I'm Dr. Gabriel Mason. I hope I haven't kept you waiting long."

"Not at all," Davison replies coolly. "Now just tell me how you're going to make my wife better."

Ignoring my husband's blunt remark, I watch as Dr. Mason sits down at his desk, pulls out my file and films, then clasps his hands together and looks at me straight in the eye. "Allegra, you have suffered a vocal fold hemorrhage. One of the blood vessels in your vocal cords burst, which caused you to cough up the blood after you came offstage. Did you experience any symptoms before the rupture?"

Now I feel like the stupidest person on the planet. Davison glances over at my phone as I type out, *I've had some neck pain, and my dresser said my voice sounded a bit hoarse last night.*

I hold up my phone to Dr. Mason. I'm so thankful to have my phone back. I had texted the stage manager on Davison's phone last night to allow Tomas to go into my dressing room and get my things for me, which Lucy brought over to the hospital while I was asleep.

Dr. Mason reads what I wrote and nods. "Yes, those are some of the symptoms."

Davison speaks up. "Where do we go from here?"

The doctor places his hands flat on the desk, leaning in closer to me. "First, Allegra, you must have complete vocal rest for the next two weeks. You cannot utter one single word. I mean it. From now on, write everything out as you've been doing to communicate."

Davison's grip on my hand tightens as the doctor continues.

"Then you will require about a month of voice therapy. After that, we'll reassess to determine if further action is required."

"What kind of 'further action' are we talking about?" Davison asks for me.

"Laser surgery to get rid of the vessel that initially caused the rupture."

A wave of goose bumps pop up on my arms. I look over at Davison, whose eyes soften when he stares back at me. "It's just a last resort, baby, but I'm sure it won't come to that."

I take a deep breath and write, *When can I go home?*

Dr. Mason gives me a quick grin. "You can go home today, Allegra. I'll see you in two weeks, after you've rested your voice, and then assign you a vocal therapist. But you'll also have to contact the Met and let them know your understudy will have to take over the rest of your run. And, personally, I'm so sorry to tell you that because I read your amazing reviews from opening night."

"That's all right, Doctor. Allegra will be back up on the stage before we know it, right, baby?" Davison announces, gripping my hand as my heart melts from my husband's encouragement and his love for me, which he is never embarrassed to express publically.

I nod, then the three of us rise to our feet. Davison and I take turns shaking the doctor's hand. "Thank you so much, Dr. Mason," Davison tells him.

"Of course, Mr. Berkeley. Please call me for anything at all. And, Allegra, remember…"

I motion to my lips with my hands, pretending I'm zipping them shut.

"Excellent," Dr. Mason replies, looking pleased with me.

Davison walks me out holding my hand, which I'm grateful for because I can't feel my feet under me. He quickly pulls me over to the side in the hallway. He cups my face with his strong hands and locks his eyes on mine.

"I know you're scared, baby. It's going to be okay. I swear to you. I'm going to take care of everything. Nothing but the best doctors and treatment for you, whatever it costs. You come first, and I'm going to take care of you. I don't want you to worry. I just want you well. Got it?"

Tears run softly down my face as I nod in gratitude and sheer love for my husband. I lean my forehead on his, letting his strong, hard body support me.

"We've got this, Venus. You and me," he whispers roughly. He kisses my forehead, then takes my hand. "Come on, let's get you home."

I wrap my arm around my husband's waist and cradle my head in the crook of his shoulder as he leads me back to my room so I can start packing.

* * *

Davison

I step into the apartment from the elevator, reading an urgent text from Christoph:

Hey, man, I found something incredible that you must see in Hong Kong. The returns would be huge for both of us. Get here ASAP—C

I sigh at Christoph's unfortunate timing when I hear the sounds of a sad tune being played on the piano filling the room that capture my attention. I think it's Chopin, but I can't really tell. Dressed in her sweats, Allegra is sitting on the bench, her head bent over as she focuses on the notes. I freeze on the spot, watching her, not wanting to interrupt her.

The two weeks when she couldn't talk were probably some of the worst times in my life, right up there with her kidnapping. The pain I felt for her was even more acute because unlike when that pig Morandi took her from me, this time I could actually see the hurt and pain in her face, her frustration at not being allowed to talk or sing. Frankly, I think it was more difficult for her not being able to sing than talk. We left notepads and pens all over the apartment so she wouldn't have to carry one with her everywhere. Even though she wasn't part of the production anymore, she still refrained from foods that she didn't eat when she had to sing onstage, such as dairy, alcohol, and caffeine. She became vigilant about her health, making sure we had more fruits and vegetables in the house. I cooked her salmon steaks for the omega-3, which she loved. Her father, my mother, and Lucy were frequent visitors.

Now she had a vocal therapist for the next month, who worked with her to gain her vocal strength back while allowing her voice to heal properly. Some of the techniques seemed somewhat dubious to me when I looked them up. One of them is called "digital laryngeal manipulation," which is basically when the therapist massages the patient's larynx. To me, it looked like choking, but hopefully, Allegra's therapist knew what she was doing. And for my peace of mind, I'm glad she was assigned a female therapist, because the image of another man's hands on my wife's throat— yeah, that shit would not have sat well with me at all.

The lack of music being played brings me back to the present moment. Allegra hasn't moved from the piano. And then I realize what she was playing. It was the section from *La Bohème* when Mimi and Rodolfo sing together in the falling snow at the end of Act III, vowing to stay together until spring comes. My heart instantly breaks at the recognition, and I pick up my pace toward her, watching as she runs her hands over the smooth keys.

I approach her slowly. "Hi, baby," I gently greet her.

"Hi," she whispers in return.

Ever since Allegra came home from the hospital, I've used a soft voice with her, and she has done the same since she got the all clear that she was allowed to speak again because she didn't want to risk injuring herself further. So, if my wife whispers, so do I.

I run my hand over Allegra's silky brown hair. "How was your day? Therapy session go well?"

"As well as can be expected. I just hope it helps."

"I'm sure it will. We just need to think positively. Want me to heat something up for dinner?"

She shakes her head. "No, let me do it. At least it'll feel like I'm doing something productive. I'll make a salad too."

Allegra pushes back from the piano, giving me a soft kiss on the lips before shuffling to the kitchen in her slippers.

At that instant, my mind is made up. I walk down the hallway to our bedroom and shut the door so Allegra can't hear me. I pull out my phone and scroll for Christoph's number. My message goes straight to his voice mail. "It's Davison. I got your text. I'm going to send Ian Parker, my number two, to meet you in Hong Kong. He is very good at what he does and I trust him implicitly. I apologize in advance, but my wife needs me at home. We'll talk soon."

After I hang up, I call Ian, who picks up on the second ring. "Davison, everything okay?"

"No. I need you to fly to Hong Kong tomorrow to meet with Christoph. Apparently, he's found some amazing investment opportunity, but coming from him, that could mean just about anything. I have no fucking idea what it is, but I need you to check it out and report back to me. Allegra needs me at home. You can take my jet. I'll call Teterboro and make all the arrangements."

"Of course. Whatever you need. I'll take care of it," he reassures me.

"I know you will. I left a message with Christoph, so he knows you're the one he'll be meeting with. Just send him a quick e-mail with your details once you know where you're staying."

"Don't worry. I've got it covered. Just take care of Allegra."

"That's the plan. Keep me posted."

"Will do."

I put my phone down just as Allegra pokes her head in the door. "Dinner's ready."

I nod. "Thanks, baby. Come here."

I fold her into my arms, burying my nose in her hair, inhaling her coconut shampoo.

"Everything okay, Harvard?" she whispers.

I shut my eyes, holding her tightly. "It is now, Venus. It is now."

Chapter 14

Allegra

Mrs. Berkeley? Did you hear what I just said? Are you all right?"

Yes, I heard you, you fucking quack.

Someone presses on my hand. "Allegra? Dr. Mason wants to know if you're okay."

Same office, same Ivy degrees, same view of midtown Manhattan. Same doctor, but not delivering the news I wanted to hear.

Davison's tight grip snaps me back as I attempt to comprehend what I was just told by the good doctor, who clears his throat before he repeats himself.

"As I said, Mrs. Berkeley, I'm not pleased with your latest results, which is why I want to schedule you for surgery as soon as possible so we can proceed with the laser photocoagulation."

"You may as well be speaking Latin, Doctor," Davison snaps at him.

Thank you, Harvard. I so needed you to do that.

"It's the laser surgery that will remove the blood vessel that ruptured causing the hemorrhage. I'll perform the surgery myself."

I hesitate before asking because I'm too afraid of the answer. "Will I be able to sing again?"

He does that hand-clasping thing that I'm starting to find really annoying. "There is the chance of complications, as with any surgery, but I'm very optimistic about your chances. Let me just check my schedule and we'll arrange everything for as soon as we can."

The doctor starts to rifle through his planner, which is lying on his desk, and I can't hold myself back any longer.

I take a deep breath to fight back the tears that are threatening to fall down my face as soon as I open my mouth, the words tumbling out of me. "I don't understand. I've done everything you told me to do. I didn't talk for weeks. You can ask my husband! I did voice therapy. I didn't smoke or drink alcohol. I rested. So why am I not healed? And what happens if the surgery isn't successful?"

Dr. Mason stops searching the pages as his eyes fall on me. "Allegra, again, about the surgery not being successful: let's just cross that bridge when we come to it."

"Cross that bridge when we come to it"? What kind of shit answer is that? This is my life's passion we're talking about!

I open my mouth to give the fucking doctor a piece of my mind, but Davison presses down on my hand even harder, forcing me to look at him. He locks his eyes onto mine, nodding his head so I'll know that he knows I'm about to lose it, but telling me to keep myself together because this is the man who can heal me physically. For better or worse, my life is in this man's hands.

I sit back, my shoulders now relaxed, which indicates to the doctor that he can continue.

"I believe you completely, Allegra. I know you did everything that was asked of you. Everyone's body is different, so it's always difficult to tell how slowly or quickly a patient will recover from an injury like this. But I can assure you that I will do everything I can to make you better and get you back up on that stage as soon as humanly possible."

I exhale, taking the doctor's words into consideration.

Okay. Give him a break. He knows what he's talking about.

"Thank you, Dr. Mason. I needed to hear that. I apologize. This has just been…"

He shakes his head. "No apologies necessary. I completely understand. My schedule is open the day after tomorrow. Does that work for you?"

I nod as my husband speaks for me again, always there for me. "That's perfect. Thank you, Doctor."

"Of course. My nurse will give you all of the forms and presurgery instructions on your way out."

Davison and I rise to our feet and bid my doctor good-bye. I barely exchange two words with Dr. Mason's nurse when she hands me the information for my surgery. Then I just start down the hallway to the elevators, my entire body shaking, walking so fast that Davison calls after me to slow down.

I don't stop until I get to the elevator bank, pounding furiously on the button. Davison finally reaches me and pulls me roughly to him.

"Baby, I know that was hard to hear, but it's going to be okay."

I struggle to get out of his hold, but he won't let go. "How do you know that, Davison?" I hiss back at him. "I did everything I was told to do, and it still wasn't good enough. What if the surgery doesn't work? What if I can't sing for the rest of my life? That's all I know. That's all I've been trained to do, what I've wanted to do my entire life. And now I'm fucked!"

I know the pain in my husband's eyes, downturned in concern and worry, reflects my own.

Just then, the elevator finally arrives. He takes hold of my shoulders and steps inside with me. Once the doors close, he turns my face to his, his eyes boring into mine.

"Baby, you are not fucked. Yes, this totally sucks, and I'm just as pissed as you are at all this. It's bullshit, plain and simple. I can barely function knowing you're going through this. I just want you to remember that no matter what happens, I will always be here for you. You need to yell, bitch, scream, shout…you aim all that crap my way, Venus, because I can take it. If it's your pain, then it's my pain too. Got it?"

My mouth starts to tremble. Within seconds, Davison takes me into his arms as I collapse into racking sobs that just keep coming and coming.

"Let go, baby," he whispers soothingly, brushing his hand over my hair over and over to calm me. "I'm here. Just let go."

I don't even notice when the elevator reaches the lobby level. I turn my head into the crook of Davison's shoulder. "I can't…"

His warm breath trails across my ear. "Just walk with me, baby. You don't have to look at anybody."

I don't think I've been more grateful for my husband than at this exact moment as he leads me to the Maybach waiting outside on the corner and bundles me carefully inside.

* * *

When we walk into our building, I spot Lucy sitting on one of the leather sofas in the marble lobby. She gets to her feet when she sees Davison and me, making her way to us.

Her eyes pop out of their sockets. I can only imagine what I look like right now. "Oh my God, Alli, are you okay?"

I blow my nose again. "I'll be fine, thanks to my husband."

I glance over at Davison, who leans over to kiss my head. "What's up?"

"Can we talk?" she asks sheepishly.

"Of course. Let's go sit by the river. I need some fresh air."

I wait for Davison to object, but he simply kisses me softly on the lips and says, "I'll be upstairs."

I watch him walk away to our private elevator, giving me a huge smile and mouthing, *Love you*, before the doors close.

"So, what's going on with you?" Lucy asks. And I fill her in on all of my news as we walk to the Esplanade along the Hudson.

We settle onto a bench with a direct view of the Statue of Liberty and Ellis Island.

I turn to face my best friend. "Okay, your turn. Talk to me."

She looks at me straight in the eyes. "I'm pregnant."

I knew it.

I sigh, placing my hand on her arm in concern. "Are you sure?"

She snorts. "I'd say ten pregnancy tests and throwing up anything that resembles food pretty much says it all."

I lean back on the bench. "That explains your mood swings and those weird eating habits, like you had at my dress fitting."

"Yeah," she whispers. "I had my suspicions then, but I wasn't sure until my period never showed up."

I swallow in my throat, hoping she won't be upset about my admission. "I thought the same thing."

She exhales and nods. "It's okay, Alli. I guess I just didn't want it to be true."

"Oh, honey. What did Tomas say?"

"I don't know, since I haven't told him yet."

My mouth drops. "Lucy, you have to tell him!"

"Well, that would be difficult since he's in the Czech Republic and I have no idea when he's coming back," she informs me.

My mouth drops farther at this news. "What? Is he there to see his family?"

"I would think so, but he was so vague about it. He just announced a few days ago that he was going—no advance notice, nothing."

"And you don't know when he's coming back?"

She shakes her head. "Nope." Her voice turns quiet as she begins to cry. "How do I tell him, Alli? I have no idea how he'll react. He's been so sensitive about everything, especially my friendship with Ian. No matter how many times I try to reassure him, he doesn't believe that we're just friends and nothing more. So how the hell do you think he'll take it when I tell him I'm pregnant?"

I take Lucy's hand in mine. "This is what you're going to do. When he comes back, you sit him down and tell him. And if he doesn't believe you, then he's not worth the effort. But I think he is. We had a long talk at the engagement party."

She pulls out a tissue from her coat pocket and wipes her nose. "You did?"

Sorry, Tomas. You had your chance. My best friend is a wreck, and she comes first.

I inhale deeply. "You're gonna kill me for this…"

"Doubtful."

"I overheard your argument with him when you told him to drop the woe-is-me look."

She shakes her head at me. "Shit, Alli, why didn't you tell me this before?"

"Didn't think you'd appreciate knowing that. But there's more. I talked to Tomas after he came out of the room."

Lucy sits up in attention. "What did he say?"

"He's worried about what you think of him and his family."

Her eyebrows narrow in confusion. "What *about* his family? I've never met them."

"That's the point. After what he said, I doubt you ever will because he's afraid of what you'll think of them." I wait to let her take in what I just said. "Sweetie, do you know what they do for a living?"

"No," she whispers.

"His father is a farmer and his mom's a schoolteacher."

"So what?" she screeches.

"That's the point I tried to make with him. You wouldn't care what they do. But you also have to see this from his point of view. Your father is a big shot in the art world and makes a lot of money. How could he possibly measure up to that?"

She starts to cry harder now. "But he does. I don't care who his parents are. I love him for him. He makes me laugh. He respects me. And he gives me mind-blowing orgasms."

I roll my eyes. "Too much information, there, sweetie. But I get it. So when he gets back, tell him everything that you just said, listen to him, and then let him know he's going to be a daddy. And I bet you anything he'll be ecstatic."

Lucy nods her head. "I hope so. And for the record, I'm not mad anymore."

I exhale in relief. "Good. Now, have you been to see an ob-gyn yet?"

She wipes her eyes. "I have an appointment next week. I was going to ask you if you'd come with me, but you'll be a little busy."

"Yeah, unfortunately. But, if Tomas turns out to be a shit, which I highly doubt, then I'll be your Lamaze coach. You're my best friend, and we're in this together. And you have to start taking prenatal vitamins and lots of folic acid. I have to look out for my future godchild, you know."

"I know, and—"

"No more alcohol, caffeine, sushi, smoking…"

"Since when have you ever seen me smoke?"

"No soft cheeses, no overindulging on junk food…"

Lucy holds up her hands to me, palms facing out. "Stop! Shit, Alli, I think I liked it better when you couldn't talk."

I smile back at her. "Ha-ha. Very funny."

Her eyes begin to fill again with tears. "No matter what happens, we'll be there for each other."

I slide over closer to my best friend, hugging her firmly. "Always."

Chapter 15

Davison

It's true what people say—time always seems to stop in a hospital. Whenever I look up to check the clock on the wall of Allegra's hospital room, the hands don't appear to have moved. I just want, I *need*, someone to come out here and tell me that she's okay, that the operation is going smoothly, but nobody has appeared yet to deliver any news to me, and I'm about ready to lose my mind.

I glance around the room and can't help but smile at all of the flowers that have arrived for her so soon. We checked her in at nine a.m., she was in the OR by ten, and two hours later, there are enough bouquets in this small space to resemble a shop in the Flower District—white orchids from Signora Pavoni, red tulips from Lucy, sunflowers from Derek and Aaron, and pink roses from La Diva, ordered all the way from her villa in Italy. But I made sure my apricot roses for her were placed in a prominent spot, right next to the eight-by-ten picture of us from our wedding day in a Tiffany frame that usually sits on our mantel at home, which I brought with me, unbeknownst to her. I want it to be the first thing she sees when she's back in her room.

My phone vibrates inside my breast jacket pocket. Ian's name flashes on the caller ID.

"Hey, how is Hong Kong?" I ask. "Everything going okay with Christoph?"

"Yeah, it's all good. He's fine. But, Christ, can that man drink me under the table!"

I laugh from the memory of him doing that to me when we were younger. "I see things never change. Tell me more about this investment opportunity."

"Actually, there're a bunch of them that he's interested in; some aren't too legit as far as I can tell, but there's one that I think would interest you as well. Voice telecommunications."

"Really? I was interested in something like that back when I still ran Berkeley Holdings. I was supposed to fly to Shanghai, but the deal fell through. Get me the specifics, because if the same team is involved, I think it's something that would be good for DCB."

"You got it. How's Allegra doing?"

"She's in surgery now. Hopefully, I'll hear something soon."

"Sending her positive thoughts, Davison."

"Thanks, Ian. Means a lot." A *beep* signals an incoming call. "Gotta go. I've got Christoph on the other line."

"Well, well...look who finally decided to wake up." Ian snorts.

"I'd better take this. I'm pleased to hear it's going well."

"Yup, no worries, Davison. I'll get you that info ASAP. And keep me posted on Allegra."

"Thanks, Ian. Will do. Talk later."

I end my call with Ian and switch over to Christoph.

"Christoph, I was just talking to Ian."

"Oh, man, that Ian." He laughs. "You've got a good one there, Berkeley. He knows his shit. Reminds me of you."

"Thanks. I'll take that as a compliment. So, no complaints? Anything you need from me?"

"No, man. It's good. I'm showing him a good time. He's never been to Hong Kong before, so we're going to hit the casinos on Macau tonight."

Oh fuck.

"Well, enjoy yourselves, and take it easy on him, okay?"

"No worries, man. *Ciao.*"

I fall back in my chair, sighing a breath of relief. Christoph seems to be pleased, and Ian is doing his job brilliantly. At least one area of my life is running smoothly.

Suddenly, the door opens, and a nurse walks in. "Mr. Berkeley, I was told to tell you that your wife's operation is going well and there are no complications so far."

Oh, thank God. Thank God. Thank God.

My shoulders drop, and I exhale deeply.

"Thank you for telling me. Do you know how much longer it'll be?"

"I'm afraid I don't."

I nod. "Thank you. I'll be here in case anything else comes up."

"Of course."

Once the nurse is gone, I drop my head into my hands, my elbows on my knees. "Please, God, let her be okay. Just let her be okay. Don't let anything happen to her. You can do whatever you want to me; I don't care. Have me shot again, I can take it. That bullet was nothing. A fucking pinprick. Just bring her back to me."

I lift my head and take a deep breath. Time to call her father and my mom, and text everyone else that so far, my Allegra, my

strong, beautiful, courageous wife with the smart mouth, is holding her own.

* * *

Allegra

I open my eyes and nobody is in the room. Not even Davison,
who's been sitting guard at my bedside ever since I was brought
back from recovery. But at least from where I'm lying in bed, I
can see him, thanks to the wedding picture he brought from
home without telling me. That and the apricot roses were the
first things I saw when I was wheeled back in, and the last things
I saw before I went to sleep.

Everyone has taken turns visiting me—Papa, Mrs. Berkeley,
Lucy, Derek, and Aaron, though it was sometimes difficult with
those two, since they always make me laugh and I'm not allowed
to talk because my larynx needs to heal. But I can see all of their
glorious flowers, which make me feel somewhat better, having
them with me.

I'm still waiting to hear something concrete from Dr. Mason
about my condition. He said the surgery went well with no complications, but to me, that only means that he didn't need to get
out the paddles and shock me back to life.

I reach over carefully for some water, but my cup is empty, as
is the pitcher. I press the call button for the nurse and wait. And
wait.

After ten minutes, I can't take it anymore. My throat is
parched. I slowly slide out of bed, rolling my IV stand with me
to the door. I turn left to head for the nurses' station when two
voices stop me. The male voices belong to Dr. Mason and another

man in a white coat, who I assume is also a doctor. They're standing outside the room next door to mine, their backs to me. I
know I shouldn't eavesdrop, but as soon as Dr. Mason says the
word "singer," I freeze.

"Too much scarring. It was worse than I thought it would be,"
Dr. Mason tells the other man.

"Poor thing. So young. I've seen it happen with rock singers too.
Opera is so tough, though. Do you think she'll ever sing again?"

Dr. Mason pauses. "Not professionally, no. Allegra is so talented. I just don't know how I'll break it to her."

You just did, asshole.

I start to tremble as I ease backward into the room. I can hear
someone howling in the distance, and I realize it's me.

I collapse to the ground, gulping oxygen by the lungful. I press
my hand over my mouth, as if that will stop my screaming.

No! That fucker said he would fix me!

No! No! No!

A rush of heat blazes through me. Rage. I want to rage.

"NO! NO! NO!" I shout, my throat in flames, pain shooting
down my neck into my lower body.

I get up from the floor and kick my IV stand to the floor, completely impervious to the pain as the fall snatches out the needle
from my arm, blood spattering all over the pristine floor. My larynx is on fire as I knock over the chairs, screaming at the top of
my lungs.

*I won't be singing professionally anymore, so who gives a fuck if I
mess up my throat? I sure don't give a shit.*

I hurl my pillow across the room, bringing down the wall
clock. I throw one of the bouquets against the door, petals and
water covering the floor.

I rage. I rage. I rage. And it feels fucking amazing.

I rage against the strong arms holding me back. I rage like a trapped animal as someone shouts, "Allegra! Stop! Calm down!" Writhing and kicking with every limb on my body as a needle is shoved into my arm, I hear Davison's voice shouting above everyone else's, "Let me hold her! I'm her fucking husband!"

Then my world turns liquid and quiet as Davison lifts me into his arms and places me on the bed, whispering, "I'm here, baby. I'm here. I love you so much. I'll never leave you again."

I float away on his words into sleep, my body boneless and free of pain.

* * *

I'm never leaving this bed. Ever.

From my bedroom window, I watch day turn into night, and night turn into day.

There's no point in rising from this bed. I will never sing again. I am useless. I have nothing to give to anyone. Davison will no doubt see what kind of loser of a woman he married and leave me. Can't say I would blame him. I'd leave me too.

I don't understand why he keeps leaving me food. The tea eventually goes cold. The meat in the sandwiches spoils. Such a waste, just like me.

Papa comes by every day. "*Cara*," he whispers, smoothing my hair back from my face. He says things like "Please get up," "Please eat something," "Please say something."

Please. Please. Please. Please, fucking please.

Then Lucy visits me. She tries to make me laugh, telling me stories about Tomas, her parents, even the latest Hollywood gossip. She doesn't get it either. I could care less.

But Davison…Davison is the worst because it hurts the most.

It's his pity. He emits it through his words, everything that comes from his mouth. It permeates my pores when he touches me. I shiver from the feel of his fingers on my flesh. But when he kisses me…I want to slap him.

Don't! Just fucking don't! I know you hate me. I know you think I'm a complete loser. Go back to Ashton. Or find another WASP princess who will do you proud. I'm not worth it.

I wait for the day when he'll present me with divorce papers. I will snatch the pen from his hands and scratch out my signature at those yellow tabs that say SIGN HERE and SIGN HERE and SIGN HERE—I'll sign wherever you fucking want me to sign.

I will go back and live with Papa. I know Davison will take back the money he promised him, so I don't know where we'll end up. Maybe we'll go back to Italy and live there. I'll find a job, maybe teach English. Papa will find us a small apartment to live in for him and his divorcée daughter, but we wouldn't tell anyone I'm divorced, since divorce is frowned upon there. A widow. Yes, that would work better. I wouldn't want to bring any more shame to him than I already have.

Suddenly, Davison walks into the bedroom. My body locks, afraid of his touch, not wanting to feel his hands on me. I don't want to feel anything. Not a damn thing.

He shoves the handheld phone in front of my face. "It's Saxon, baby. He insists on speaking with you. I keep trying to put him off, but being the bastard he is, he won't take no for an answer."

Davison holds the phone up to my ear, thank God. I couldn't bear it if his fingers brushed mine when he handed it to me.

"Allegra?" Jared's rough voice shouts over the line.

"Yes," I manage, barely above a whisper.

He sighs audibly. "Look, I hate to do this, but I have no choice."

Christ, just get to the damn point already.

"Allegra, I have to drop you as a client. With your doctor's diagnosis, I don't see the point of keeping you on. And I know I've been an asshole at times with you, but please believe me when I tell you this is without a doubt the hardest thing I've ever had to do in my life. I had such dreams for you…"

Join the fucking club.

"…and now, it just breaks my fucking heart."

He pauses, and I start to think he actually means what he's saying, but it really doesn't matter now.

"I'll have to send you an official letter as per your contract."

"Fine," I reply.

"I'm so sorry, Allegra," he rushes. "I truly am. Be well. Good-bye."

He hangs up, thank God. I turn onto my other side, away from Davison's hand holding the phone.

"Bastard!" Davison growls under his breath. Then I feel his warm hand on my shoulder. "Allegra, please. Talk to me."

I shut my eyes tightly, wrapping my arms around me, shrinking away from his touch and burrowing farther under the covers.

I hear him sigh in frustration. "Just remember I love you, baby, and I'm not going anywhere."

Retreating footsteps echo through the bedroom, followed by the sound of a closing door.

Leave me alone. Just leave me alone! I don't want your pity or your love. Stop hovering! And stop playing this game, pretending you care about me! Just come in and tell me it's over. Clean and swift. Then I can move on and forget you ever came into my life.

And after he does that, I can finally leave everything behind—this bed, this life, and everything Davison Cabot Berkeley ever meant to me.

Chapter 16

Davison

One month later...

Staring out the living room window in our apartment that looks out onto the Hudson River, I watch the various forms of water traffic sailing up and down it. Sheets of rain pound against the glass, the sky gray and overcast, all of which perfectly matches my mood. I wouldn't have been able to stand it if the sky had been a brilliant blue, cloudless, with the sun beaming down on me.

I turn and step to the piano, running a finger across the ebony wood. I check the tip of it, now covered entirely in dust. I can't remember the last time I heard someone playing it, the someone being my beautiful wife. I wouldn't care if she played something sad and haunting; I just need her to do something, to show some sign of life.

My phone buzzes from the coffee table. Christoph's name is on the screen.

"Hi, Christoph," I manage to muster.

"Hey, man. How are you? How is Allegra?"

I swallow deeply in my throat before answering. "She's doing fine. What can I do for you?"

"I've got something I want to check out in Dubai. Any chance you can come out?"

I take a deep breath before answering. "I'm afraid not. I really need to stay with Allegra. I'll send Ian, if that's all right with you. He's basically running the company now for me while I tend to her."

"No problem. I like Ian. We had the best time in Hong Kong. And that girl of his, Ashton...How do you Americans say? A total pistol."

My eyebrows furrow in confusion. "Wait. Ashton who? She was with Ian?"

"Oh shit, man!" Christoph interrupts. "My plane's boarding, Davison. We'll talk soon, yeah?"

He hangs up before he can give me an answer to my question. It couldn't be...

Before I can process this information, the house phone rings. "Sir, Ashton Canterbury is downstairs. She'd like to see you and Mrs. Berkeley," our doorman informs me.

I sigh. "Fine, send her up."

What now?

I tilt my head in curiosity when Ashton steps out of the elevator, not just because she's carrying a large shopping bag from Dean & Deluca, but also because she's not the Ashton I remember. She's wearing a black silk wrap dress, tall stiletto boots, and a red belted raincoat.

"Ashton," I greet her coolly. "What are you doing here?"

"I heard about Allegra, and—"

I don't like this, not one bit. "What did you hear exactly?" I demand of her before she can say another word.

She pauses before answering. "I heard that she lost her voice and can't sing professionally anymore."

"From who?"

"People talk, okay? Especially in our circles. Look, it doesn't matter—"

I take a step toward her as a warning. "It matters to me, because I will not allow you to come near Allegra if your intention is to hurt her!"

Her jaw clenches. "Did Allegra tell you that I saw her before the wedding?"

This news sends me reeling. "No. Where?"

"She'd just had her dress fitting at Maggie's. I ran into her on the street outside. I told her that I'm sorry you were shot, that I was sorry for all of the trouble I caused her, and I wished you both well."

"If you don't mind, Ashton, I think I'll ask Allegra about that just to confirm it's true."

"Look, Davison, I'm not the same person anymore." She huffs. "I know you may find that difficult to believe, but it's true. I've met someone who's changed me for the better, and I'm much happier now."

I give her a once-over, silently admitting to myself that she's not lying. "You've definitely changed. I think your mother will freak out seeing you in red and black with no pearls in sight."

"Actually, she did," she replies, now beaming with pride, "and I told her she'd just have to accept me for who I am." She offers the shopping bag to me. "This is for you and Allegra. I thought flowers would be too depressing, so I brought you some things from Dean and Deluca that I remembered you liked and other stuff that I hope is to Allegra's taste."

I take the bag from her, looking down at it, weighing it in my hand as well as what my response should be to this random act of kindness. "I guess you have changed, because I don't think the Ashton I knew would've done something like this, at least not the version when we were engaged. You're different, almost like the girl I first met—funny and kind, before we grew up and became such…"

"Narcissistic, self-absorbed, materialistic assholes?"

I let out a big laugh. "Yeah, that. Allegra has changed me for the better."

"So has my new man. Just call me Ashton 2.0," she jokes. "Look, I'd better go. Please give Allegra my best. I can't tell you how sorry I am that this happened to her. Truly I am."

I nod. "Thank you, Ashton. And I believe you."

I give her a quick hug before she presses for the elevator. Once Ashton is gone, I rush to the bedroom to share everything that's just happened with Allegra. But when I reach her, she's asleep, and the joy I felt looking forward to sharing this piece of gossip with her dissipates into thin air.

She has taken up permanent residence in the bedroom. She hardly ever leaves it. Whenever I check on her, she is either sleeping or awake staring into space. Her appetite is nonexistent; the food she takes in, if she eats at all, could barely feed a baby bird.

I come around to her side of the bed where a letter lies on the ground, torn in half. I know what it said before she ripped it up.

Dear Allegra,

As per our conversation, our professional relationship is hereby terminated according to section 5, paragraph 3 in your contract.

Sincerely,
Jared Saxon
President
Saxon Management

The bastard dropped her, and he didn't even do it in person. He did it over the fucking phone. I wanted to kill him, just like I did after I found out she'd heard about her damaged larynx thanks to that fucking Dr. Mason's tactlessness. I wanted to rip his own larynx out because his big mouth caused Allegra's meltdown, the one where I had to restrain her so a nurse could inject her with a drug that would knock her out. I'd never seen her like that before. I hated myself for leaving her, even just for a second. I just slipped out for a minute to collect some things from Charles that I'd asked him to bring over from home, and, not wanting him to have to park the car, I met him outside the hospital. When I came back and was walking down the corridor, I heard these raw screams coming from Allegra's room, and when I came in, I found her tearing up the room and all of its contents. I yelled for help, and finally a nurse appeared with a needle in her hand, ready to jab Allegra with it. She slept soundly for hours after that, and I never left her side again.

Allegra wanted to put everything behind her, and I was fine with that. She calls the shots now. Whatever she wants to do, I'll abide by her decision one hundred percent.

My beautiful, talented wife will never sing again on the stage of the Met, or ever at La Scala and Covent Garden, as she once told me she'd dreamed of doing one day. Her larynx is scarred beyond repair, and there is nothing modern medicine or prolonged voice rest can do. Allegra is shattered, a shell of her former self. My Allegra, with the smart mouth, the smile that always made my heart stop when I saw it across her gorgeous face, the infectious laugh that inevitably made me lose it when I heard it: they're all gone, and I have no fucking clue how to get them back.

I hear the *ding* of the elevator. I wander over to the foyer, finding Lucy taking off her coat, holding her soaked umbrella carefully so as not to damage the wood.

"Hey, Lucy," I whisper.

She gives me a quick hug. "How is she?"

"The same. How are you feeling?"

She rubs her belly. "We're good. Finally. That's what I've come to tell Allegra."

"You know where to find her," I murmur. "I'll give you some privacy."

Without warning, Lucy takes my hand. "It's okay, Davison. You should hear this as well."

I dump her wet umbrella in the kitchen sink and follow her to the bedroom.

"Hey, Alli," she greets her, barely above a whisper. Lucy sits down at the edge of the bed, nudging Allegra's feet to make room for herself. I lean against the door frame, my heart pounding, to see how Allegra reacts.

Allegra's eyes shift over to Lucy, blank and lifeless. "Hi."

I envy Lucy. I can barely get a greeting out of my wife, but at least she acknowledged her best friend.

"I have some good news," Lucy begins carefully. "Tomas came back from his trip, and I told him about the baby."

"Good," Allegra replies, her voice monotone as she looks out the window.

"He finally opened up to me, and you won't believe what he's been keeping from me."

Lucy pauses before continuing. With no reaction from Allegra, she continues.

"He told me he was once married before. It was his childhood sweetheart and they had a baby together who died soon after childbirth. He was devastated. They decided to get divorced, and that's when he left the Czech Republic and came to America to start over. He's excited about the baby but nervous that something might go wrong. Can't blame him for that. But we're doing much better. We talked everything out, and we've never been happier. Just thought you'd want to know that."

Allegra doesn't move. She remains fixed on the outside view, as if something far more important is happening outside than hearing good news from her best friend. I clench my fists to stop myself from going over to my wife, throwing back the sheets, and pulling her upright to shake her until she shows any sign of life.

"Oh, and I told him that Ian was just a friend," she continues. "But I also admitted that I may have been subconsciously using him as a way to get a rise out of Tomas so he would talk to me, and I apologized for doing that to him. Tomas is a better person than me, thank God, because he forgave me. Bet you'd never see the day I'd do something like that, right? Admit it when I'm wrong?"

She lets out a quick self-deprecating laugh to lighten the mood. But, again, no reaction from my wife.

Lucy rises from the bed and steps over closer to Allegra, kneeling down to eye level with her.

"Okay, Allegra, it's time for some tough love," she declares, her voice strong and determined. "I know you need time to heal, but this is getting ridiculous. I'm your best friend, and you know I don't sugarcoat anything. So here it is. Life really sucks sometimes, and what happened to you is just beyond unfair. It's not fucking right. After everything that you've done, all of it has gone to shit, and except for you, nobody is more pissed than me, because I always knew you were meant to go far with that voice. But now you can't, and you're coming to terms with that. And that's fine. You just have to remember that you have people in your life who love you unconditionally and will always be there for you no matter what. They're hurting too, because you are, and they just want you to let them in."

Lucy stops and glances in my direction, then shifts back to Allegra.

"Alli, look at Davison."

My wife doesn't move an inch.

"Damn it, Allegra, look at your husband!" she shouts.

Finally, Allegra acknowledges me. Her head turns in my direction, her eyes locking on mine.

"Do you see him? Do you really see him? His eyes are sunken; he probably hasn't had a good sleep in ages. He hasn't shaved in days. He looks downright ragged because he's worried about you and he doesn't know how to help you."

"He can't help me. Nobody can."

Lucy's eyes pop out of their sockets, and I know mine have as well. The first full sentence that has crossed her lips in days, and it slays me to my core.

I walk away, stomping down the hallway. I get to the kitchen and pull out a crystal tumbler, filling it with Glenlivet. My nerve endings are pulsing with frustration and anger, and as much as I want to, I can't take it out on my wife.

I take a long sip of it, allowing the alcohol to burn my throat as it goes down. I inhale a lungful of oxygen, leaning against the kitchen counter to steady myself.

Lucy suddenly appears in the door frame. "I would ask you for a glass of that, but I'm not allowed."

"With good reason," I note.

She smiles wistfully. "I know." She pauses. "I tried, Davison."

I sigh. "Thank you for that. I just don't know what to do anymore. It's been a fucking month, and I understand this is so much for her to deal with, but, Jesus Christ, Luciana, I want my wife back! I want her to joke with me, to curse me out, to kiss me—fuck, I'll take anything at this point!"

Luciana pushes me farther into the kitchen, away from the hallway. "Shh! Keep your voice down! She'll come around, Davison. I know she will. Just be patient."

"You didn't sound that patient with her just now," I remind her.

"Because she needed to hear it from me. If you said to her what I just did, it would kill her. I'm not the love of her life. What she needs from you is caring and understanding, not a fucking wake-up call."

She was right. Just then, the elevator rings again, this time depositing my mother and Allegra's father, carrying two grocery bags.

"Look who I ran into!" my mother exclaims.

"I convinced Mona to help me cook dinner for you and Allegra," Mr. Orsini announces with a smile. "Luciana, how lovely to see you!"

He and my mother exchange pleasantries with Lucy as I get her coat from the closet. Once I help put it on her, she goes back to the kitchen to grab her umbrella. Before pressing for the elevator, she turns to me and takes hold of my arm.

"She'll come around, Davison. I know it. Just be there for her and call me if you need anything at all."

I nod and peck her on the cheek. "I will. And thank you again for trying."

"My pleasure. I'll see you soon."

When I go back to the kitchen, my mom is unpacking the groceries, Allegra's father nowhere to be seen. "Where's Mr. Orsini?" Then I pause, shaking my head. "Never mind. Stupid question."

Mom puts down the boxes of pasta and takes me in her arms, a cloud of Chanel No. 5 wafting around her. "How are you doing, darling?"

"As best I can. Lucy tried to talk some sense into Allegra just now, but it didn't seem to work."

"Give it time, son. This has been incredibly hard for her. Imagine someone telling you that you couldn't do what you love anymore. Singing was her life. I can't imagine what she's going through. She'll come around."

Just as those last words escape my mother's mouth, Mr. Orsini appears in the doorway of the kitchen with his arm around Allegra's shoulders.

My heart leaps into the air like a fucking rocket. She's up. She's out of the bedroom. My eyes turn moist at the sight of my beautiful wife taking the first steps.

I slowly walk to her, desperate to fold her into my arms. I gently take hold of her waist with one arm while cradling her head with the other.

"Hi, baby," I whisper into her ear.

"Hi, Harvard," she manages to reply.

I want to shout with joy, but I restrain myself.

She's finally coming back to me. My Venus.

I lean back to look into her eyes, gesturing with my head to the living room. "Come on. Let's go sit down."

She nods, and with her hand firmly in mine, I walk her over to the sofa, settling her onto my lap once I sit down.

I tuck a loose strand of her hair back behind her ear, smoothing it lovingly. "Want some music? Chopin?"

"'Raindrop,'" she whispers.

I smile slightly because it's her favorite Chopin piece. Another victory.

I glance out the window. "Kind of fitting for today, right?"

She smiles at my cheesy attempt at a joke. "Yes."

I reach for the remote on the coffee table. The quiet piano notes begin to fill the room. Allegra nestles her head into the crook of my shoulder, and I softly kiss her hair, reveling in this moment that I feared so often would never happen.

I hold my wife in my arms, enjoying the genius of Chopin. "Can you play this?"

Her body stiffens in my arms. "Now?"

Oh crap.

"No, no," I quickly correct myself. "I mean in general."

"Oh," she replies, her body loosening in relief at my explanation. "I could, but very badly." She allows herself a quiet self-deprecating laugh.

I shut my eyes, placing another kiss on her silky hair.

Please don't let this end.

Suddenly, a deep, booming laugh erupts from the kitchen, after which I can hear my mother's giggle, which I haven't heard in ages. Allegra and I turn our heads in the direction of the kitchen. I can see Mr. Orsini attempting to get my mother to taste something in a long wooden spoon, with her rearing back in protest, shaking her head. Finally, she relents and takes a small bite of whatever he is offering her. She nods her head, and I can see her reach for his hand to take another bite from the spoon.

I smile to myself, pleased to see my mother so happy and laughing, but when I look at Allegra, her jaw is fixed and her eyes have hardened as she looks on at the scene in the kitchen between our parents.

I wince when I see the expression on her face.

Shit. Shit. Shit.

She quickly disentangles herself from my arms. "Baby, wait," I beg her.

"I'm fine, Davison," she replies quietly over her shoulder.

I watch helplessly as she slowly heads back to the bedroom, with my mom and Mr. Orsini following her with their eyes as well. They look back at me for an explanation. "She's just tired," I offer in an attempt to explain.

With a deep exhale, I heave myself off the couch and make my way to the bedroom. Allegra is back under the covers, and my heart drops.

One step forward, two steps back.

When I return to the kitchen, Mom is cleaning up the counter, while Mr. Orsini is soaking the pots and pans in the sink. Both of their faces fall when they see me. "I'm so sorry, darling. Did we do something wrong?" my mother asks gently.

I shake my head. "No. I think she's just had too much activity for one day."

"Poor thing."

Allegra's father wipes his hands on a dishtowel. "Everything is in containers, so just pop them in the microwave when you're hungry. I'll just go say good-bye to her."

Once he's gone, my mom takes me by the elbow. "Darling, you can tell me. Was it us?"

I shake my head. "I honestly don't know. I could finally feel her coming back to life, and then she was gone again. I'm thinking maybe I should call Dr. Turner, the therapist who helped her after her kidnapping, because at this point, I'm out of answers."

"That might be a good idea," my mother agrees. "There's only so much we can do."

Allegra's father reappears, and he and Mom head for the elevator. "Davison, keep an eye on her, *per favore*. *Mia cara* is lost, and we need to get her back. Let me know if you need anything at all."

I nod. "Of course. I'll see you soon."

My mother kisses me on the cheek. "I'm just downstairs."

"I know, Mom. Thanks."

Both of them give me short hugs before they step into the elevator.

A thought strikes me, and I head for the bedroom. Allegra is awake, staring again out the window.

"I'm just going to the market around the corner. Do you need anything?"

She shakes her head, and I'm just grateful she replied at all.

I grab my wallet and keys before I press for the elevator. When I get to the store, it's crowded for a Sunday afternoon. I pick up a basket and load it with a bottle of her favorite Chianti, some Baci chocolates, and a bouquet of red roses, wishing like crazy they were apricot, but red should do.

The line to pay is endless; someone's card is rejected, another customer is complaining about the price of a gallon of orange juice that is supposedly on sale. I take deep breaths to calm myself, exchanging knowing looks and eye rolls with those behind me.

I finally make it upstairs to the apartment. "I'm back!"

I put away the wine and chocolates to surprise Allegra later. I grab a vase from the living room, filling it with water, then arrange the roses as perfectly as I can.

Carrying the vase to the bedroom, I shout down the hallway, "Got a surprise for you, baby!"

I turn into the room, and nearly drop the vase. The bed is empty. I put the flowers down on the floor. "Allegra?"

I check the bathroom, but she's not inside. I check every room in the apartment, but there's no sign of my wife. I pull my phone from my jeans pocket and scroll for my mother's number.

"Mom!" I shout.

"Darling, what's wrong?"

"Is Allegra with you?"

"No. Why—"

I cut her off and race back to the bedroom. I hurl open the doors to our walk-in closet. Her suitcase is gone, along with most of her clothes. "Fuck!"

My head begins to pound, with my blood rushing to my heart. I have no idea what to do, where to start.

I tumble out of the closet, my head whirring like a fan set to high. I fall to the bed, fisting the sheets with my hands.

Get a grip. Get a fucking grip right now, asshole. Where would she go?

A spot of white flashes in my peripheral vision. I glance over at my nightstand. An envelope is propped up against the lamp with "Davison" written across it.

I leap for it, tearing it apart. A sheet of paper falls down to the floor. I grab it and read the words Allegra has left for me.

Davison,

Don't worry. I just need to be with her for a bit. Please give me that. I'll be back soon.

I love you,
Allegra

I breathe a sigh of relief because I know exactly where my wife is.

Chapter 17

Allegra

The cold marble of my mother's gravestone supports my back, which I can almost take as a metaphor for my life as it is now. I need my mother's support now more than anything, so I came to her, to the cemetery where she's buried on a hilltop overlooking Naples with a gorgeous view of the Tyrrhenian Sea and Mount Vesuvius.

Showing up on my family's doorstep was definitely something they were not expecting, but it didn't matter because I *was* family. My uncle *Zio* Edmondo and my great-aunt *Zia* Delfina were ecstatic to see me, instantly welcoming me with a huge bowl of pasta alla Genovese and an enormous piece of lemon-ricotta cake.

The next day, my cousin Gino drove me up the hill to the cemetery on his Vespa. With a sandwich, some fruit, and a bottle of water I packed for myself, I stayed with my mother all day until he came back to bring me home for dinner.

I filled my mother in on everything since I last visited her with Davison after our idyllic holiday in Venice—Davison's shooting, our wedding, debuting on the stage of the Met, and finally, the loss of my voice. I laughed with her, I cried with her, and it didn't matter that I was speaking to the air; I knew Mamma was with me the entire time. Sometimes, I got odd looks from other visitors, but once they asked me if I was all right and I explained why I was talking to the air, they understood and left me alone. I was already friends with the caretaker, Enzo, who told me I could use the toilet in his shed if I needed it.

That was yesterday. I just had my lunch—slices of salami with fresh bread that my great-aunt had brought home from the bakery, along with a nice chunk of provolone and a ripe pear. I'm starting to feel sleepy. I miss Davison and feel guilty for leaving him like I did.

"He'll understand, won't he, Mamma?" I ask her. "I just couldn't take it anymore, and seeing Papa with his mother...I just needed you, you know? But I married a smart man. Hopefully, he'll figure out where I am and know I'm safe."

I lay down on the blanket I brought with me, forming my jacket into a pillow for my head. I tuck into the gravestone as if it were my mother's embrace, and close my eyes. I'm on the cusp of sleep when I hear footsteps behind me, stopping, then starting again.

"He's here, Mamma," I tell her. *Mio marito è qui.*

I shield my eyes against the burning sun, looking up at my husband's handsome face.

* * *

Davison

"Hello, husband," my wife whispers to me softly.

"Hello, wife," I reply, extending my hand to her. She takes it and I lift her to her feet, bringing her into my arms.

Her body begins to shudder, and I hold her tighter to me. "Davison, I am so sorry for everything," she starts to cry. "I just lost myself. And I know you, Papa, and everyone were trying to help me, and I shut you all out. But I didn't know what else to do. I was in denial. And, more than anything, I want to get back to you and me, but I'm afraid that maybe I pushed you away…"

I pull her head back from my chest so I can look at her in the eyes. "Baby, you could never push me away. I just felt so helpless. When you hurt, I hurt. And it killed me that I couldn't do anything for you."

Her hands clench my jacket in fists. "I'm just so angry, Davison. Why would this happen to me? I've never done anything to deserve this… I'm so lost and I don't know where to go from here. Singing was everything to me."

I caress her face with the pads of my fingers. "We'll figure it out together, Allegra. You'll find your place in opera again. Maybe you can teach it? Or work in some capacity with the Met? But just know that no matter what happens, I will be by your side, supporting you the entire time as you figure it out."

She smiles at me through her tears. "Thank you," she chokes out.

I tug on her hands. "Come and sit with me for a bit. I'm tired. I flew all night to get here."

"When did you leave?" she asks as I pull her down with me.

"Late last night. You asked for a few days, and I respected that. But two days were all I could take being away from you."

"I know. I was starting to miss you too. Let's just be here together."

Allegra settles in my lap. I dig a tissue out of my pocket and hand it to her, then wrap my arms around her.

She wipes her eyes and blows her nose, tucking the tissue into her pocket. "I'm so sorry I just left like that. I knew you'd find my note, and hopefully you'd understand where I went."

"Of course I knew," I reply incredulously. "How could I not? I knew something was up after that look you gave my mom and your dad when they were laughing in the kitchen."

"It just floored me, seeing them like that, and it hurt because—no offense to your mom, because I adore her, but I just wish it had been Mamma who was in the kitchen with him instead."

I kiss Allegra's hair. "Of course I understand. That's only natural. I'm not offended at all. Oh, but you'll never guess who stopped by to check on you."

"Who?"

I pause. "Ashton."

She leans back to look into my eyes, her own wide in surprise. "Really?"

"Yeah, and she looked so different. She told me you ran into her before the wedding."

"I did. After my fitting at Maggie's. I wasn't going to put up with her shit, but she wished us well and was glad you were okay after the shooting. I guess whoever she's dating now has shown her the error of her ways."

I laugh. "I'll say. She was wearing red when I saw her."

Allegra settles back into me. "Yup, sounds about right. She was wearing all black when I saw her. No more WASP princess."

I slowly stroke my wife's hair. "Allegra…"

"Hmm?"

"You'd be fine with our parents spending more time together, wouldn't you?"

She sighs, tucking her head closer into my chest. "I think so. I know Mamma is gone, and I just want Papa to be happy. And if he finds that happiness with your mom, that would be okay with me."

"Good. I'm glad," I reply in relief.

We sit in silence for a bit, enjoying the feel of one another in each other's arms.

"You really did know, didn't you, Davison?" she whispers.

"What, baby?"

"Where I was."

"Of course. Didn't you think I would?"

"Yes. It just...It makes me love you even more than I thought possible. That you knew without my having to explain myself or give any more clues about where I was going."

"It'll always be like that with us. Trust me."

"I do."

"Good." I nudge my wife off my lap and rise to my feet.

She looks at me quizzically from the blanket. "What's going on?"

"I think we need to just be together, like you said. Agreed?"

"Yes," she replies suspiciously with a raised eyebrow.

"Good, because I've booked us a suite at a hotel on Capri. I want to be with you and make love to the point of exhaustion. I want to be with my wife. How does that sound to you, Mrs. Berkeley?"

Allegra stands up, tugs me to her, and kisses me long and deep. "Sounds perfect, Mr. Berkeley."

She pulls away and starts to collect her things. I fold the blanket, holding it in my arms as I watch Allegra kiss the top of her mother's grave.

"Ti amo, Mamma. Grazie."

I touch the grave as well, as a sign of respect, then take Allegra's hand, gripping it in mine as I lead her out of the cemetery to the waiting taxi, whose driver I paid handsomely to wait for me until I returned with my wife.

* * *

We bid good-bye to Allegra's relatives, who insisted we stay the night, but thankfully, Allegra was able to convince them to let us go. In my basic knowledge of Italian since Allegra came into my life, I overheard the words for "together" and "alone." I assumed those did the trick because within an hour, we were sitting on a hydrofoil speeding to the island of Capri.

A representative from the hotel was waiting for us at the dock, taking our overnight bags from us and driving us to the hilltop, where our suite was waiting for us with a basket of fruit, a chilled bottle of champagne, the entire space festooned in fresh flowers.

We took quick showers and are now lying in matching robes on the double chaise of our balcony with a gorgeous view of the sea below and the surrounding villas, champagne in hand.

I clear my throat before saying something. "Allegra, I want to sue Dr. Mason."

Her head twists to me, a look of fear across her face. "What? No, Davison. I don't want that."

"Why? He deserves it for being so callous and thoughtless."

She shakes her head vehemently. "No. I agree he was an asshole for talking about my case within earshot of my room, but he didn't cause my injury. What happened to me is nobody's fault. It just happened, and the sooner I accept that, the sooner I can move on. Please don't prolong this. I just want this behind me. But there is something you can do for me."

"Name it, baby."

"You can support me when I go back to see Dr. Turner. I think she can help me deal with all of this."

A wave of warmth washes over me.

Thank God.

I smile at her, leaning in to kiss her soundly on the lips. "Of course I'd be okay with that. I actually told your father that maybe I would bring it up with you when you're ready."

Her eyes widen in surprise. "Really? You said that?"

"Yes. Why are you so surprised?"

"It's not that I'm surprised. It just tells me how well we get each other because we were both thinking the same thing."

"Which just goes to show that I was meant to lose my glove that night at Le Bistro so I could meet the love of my life," I point out.

Allegra stares at me silently for what feels like ages, then takes my face in her hands, kissing me wet and long, as her hands begin to roam over my hair, bringing me in deeper. My dick is hard as stone within seconds when she breaks away from my mouth.

Her brown eyes lock on mine, a fiery look of lust blazing back at me. "Fuck me, Davison. Right now."

With a grunt, I roll off the chaise, lifting my wife into my arms, rushing as fast as I can back into the suite, dropping her onto the bed as I yank off my robe, falling on top of her. I dive for her mouth, devouring it as her hands grab my back, her nails digging into my skin. I trail my tongue down her throat, reaching her beautiful tits. I begin to feast on them, pushing them together so I can lick them simultaneously.

Allegra groans my name. "Oh, Davison! Fuck yes! Yes!" she exclaims. "Missed this, baby. Missed you so much...Don't stop."

"I'm just getting started, baby," I reassure her, murmuring from between her tits. "I've missed you too. Your scent, your taste. Now I'm going to suck on your clit and finger-fuck you, then I'm going to fuck you hard with my cock."

"Please, Davison," she cries out. "Do it! Do it all!"

I lick my way down her belly reaching her pussy, which is already drenched, ready for me. I dive in with my tongue, kissing her folds as if it were her mouth. I groan from the taste of her on my mouth, reveling in the feel of her again. I absently reach for one of her tits, and she takes my hand, covering her nipple as I knead her breast.

I take her clit, rolling my tongue around it. Allegra writhes helplessly on the bed, and I pull my hand back to pin her down, using my other hand to start thrusting my fingers inside her. I glance up quickly to see her head twisting back and forth, desperate for the release to come, and I will give it to her, sucking her and fucking her as fast as I can. I want my Venus to come alive. I need to hear her come.

Her muscles lock and her essence pours out of her like sweet honey, which I lick up greedily like a cat swallowing fresh milk. I slowly ease my body up to reach her mouth, where she grabs my head and clamps her mouth over mine, claiming it with a ferocity that I've never felt from her before, and it hardens my cock to the point of pain.

She purrs as she kisses me, our tongues tangling together, her hands locked on my face so I can't move, and I don't want to. I am hers, here for her pleasure. Only for her.

I pant when she finally breaks away. "You love tasting yourself on my tongue, don't you, baby?"

"Yes, Davison," she replies breathlessly.

"Good, because now you're going to have me inside you. I need to fuck you now."

"Oh God, yes," she moans as I position my cock into her

soaked pussy. I ease inside seamlessly. We mutually gasp at the feel of each other again, welcoming the familiar sense of belonging, of reminding ourselves that, yes, this is us, this is our love, this is home.

"Open your eyes, Allegra," I command my wife. "I want to see you looking at me when you yell my name again with me inside you when I'm fucking you."

Her eyes lock with mine. Her jaw is clenched, her breath increasing with each thrust of my cock. Her hands grip my ass, her fingers pinching the flesh, spurring me on. I begin to increase my speed, pounding into her as she starts to shout, her head thrown back, "Yes! Davison! Yes!"

Her inner muscles tighten around my dick like a vise. She's nearly there.

"Look at me, Allegra! Now!" I grunt.

Her eyes glance at me once before they roll back into her head as her orgasm overcomes her, my name exploding from her lips. I can feel her pussy locking on to my cock, milking it as my entire body shudders from the exquisite release.

I collapse onto Allegra's sweat-soaked body, my head next to her ear as I pant into it, her coconut-scented hair intoxicating me, its familiar smell relaxing me like an elixir. I can feel her fingers traveling up and down my back, cooling my heated flesh.

Once my heartbeat regulates, I turn onto my side, taking Allegra with me and tucking her into my body. We both yawn simultaneously, spent and sated.

"I love you, Davison," she whispers into my chest.

"I love you, Allegra," I reply, the last words I speak before we fall into blissful sleep, holding each other tightly, never letting go.

Chapter 18

Allegra

I tuck my legs under me on Dr. Turner's velvet couch. Everything looks exactly the same—same Tiffany lamp, same Persian rug, same Dr. Turner in a gauzy blouse and peasant skirt, with her silver hair pulled back into a braid.

I'm in the familiar cocoon of Dr. Turner's office, and I feel safe. I've just told her everything that's happened to me.

She nods, a contemplative look crossing her face. She folds her hands in her lap and leans toward me. "Allegra, you were in mourning."

I was not expecting this. "But nobody died," I point out to her.

She shakes her head. "You did, meaning the former version of yourself. The Allegra you were who could sing opera and had her debut at the Met, who was bound to have a successful career. That Allegra is gone."

A wave of realization comes over me. "I never thought of it that way. It never would have crossed my mind."

I sit back and allow Dr. Turner to continue.

"When you overheard your doctor discussing your diagnosis and you sank into that spiral of rage, you were angry. Then you kept to yourself away from everyone, you didn't eat, you suffered from fatigue. And now you're past all of that, accepting the reality of your situation."

"It's not like I have a choice," I point out to her. "I just wish I knew where to go from here."

"You will figure it out, Allegra. I promise you. You don't have to rush into anything. Just take things as they come. You're lucky to have such a wonderful support in Davison, your father, your friends. They will be there for you every step of the way. You just need to let them in."

I nod in understanding. "Thank you. I needed to hear that."

Dr. Turner checks her watch. "Our time is about up. Is there anything else you'd like to discuss?"

I shake my head. "No. I feel much better now. I'm just glad I came to see you. It was something I was thinking about when I was in Italy, and when I brought it up and Davison said he had thought the same thing, I knew it was time."

The doctor smiles back at me. "You see! *There* is your support system in action. You were both in total sync, which only shows how well you complement each other."

My body warms at the thought of my husband. "Yes, we certainly do."

I rise from the couch, and Dr. Turner walks me to her door, embracing me firmly before I leave. "Same time next week?" she asks.

I smile back at her. "Definitely. Thank you, Dr. Turner."

Stepping out onto the sidewalk, I'm midway through wrapping my scarf tighter around my neck when something catches my eye.

Davison is leaning against the Maybach, holding a huge arrangement of apricot roses, a huge grin across his face, his gorgeous eyes lighting up at the sight of me.

My pulse starts to race at the sight of him. "I thought you were at work."

He smirks at me. "I set my own hours. Perks of being the boss."

I step to him, taking the flowers from his hands. He wraps his arm around my waist, his warm lips covering mine as he kisses me for what seems like ages.

"Thank you, Harvard," I tell him breathlessly when we finally stop.

"My pleasure, Venus," he replies against my lips. "Now let's go home."

He helps me into the car, with Charles pulling away from the curb and heading down Seventh Avenue.

Davison curls me into his body. "How did it go with Dr. Turner?"

I recall everything to him when a strange look crosses his face. "Davison, what's wrong?"

He pauses before answering. "I did something while you were in surgery, something that's very unlike me."

"What do you mean?"

He exhales, then answers my question. "I had a one-on-one with God."

I lean back from him in surprise. "Go on."

"I told God to let you live and save your voice, and in return, I would let myself be shot again."

I shriek in horror. "What? Davison, what the hell were you thinking?"

"It didn't happen, obviously."

"No, but that's not the point," I counter. "I thought I'd lost you for good when you were shot. Why would you even think something like that? Why would you wish for something like that?"

He takes my hands in his, kissing them softly. "Because I love you, Allegra. You're my wife. I didn't want to lose you. I would've done anything to save you. I was so helpless. All the money I have was useless because it couldn't do shit for you, so I offered myself instead."

"Yeah, well, the next time you get the brilliant idea to have a quick chat with God, don't…I mean…Oh, hell, I don't know what I mean. Look, things just turned out the way they're supposed to, and there's nothing I can do about it. This is my life now, and I just have to deal with it."

He leans in and kisses my forehead. "We'll figure it out together, baby. I'm sorry I shouted."

I soften at his touch. "Me too. There actually is something we could do together."

"And that is?"

"I've been thinking about this ever since we got back. I'd like to have a party in our home, both for the holidays and as a way of thanking everyone for being there for me. And I don't want it catered, but maybe a potluck so everyone can bring their favorite food?"

Davison beams at me. "I love that idea. Let's start planning when we get home—guest list, date, the whole nine."

I pick up my roses from my side and place them on my lap, snuggling in closer to this amazing man, my husband, closing my eyes, his masculine scent that is all Davison Cabot Berkeley comforting me as we head for home.

Chapter 19

Davison

I watch my beautiful wife standing in front of the full-length mirror in our walk-in closet in four-inch gold stilettos, smoothing out her emerald-green silk dress, checking her face and hair one last time before our guests arrive.

I give her a wolf whistle. "I married one sexy woman."

"Who chose a dress that matches her smoking-hot husband's eyes," she replies, still making sure she looks presentable, which is completely unnecessary.

I step forward to her, wrapping my arms around her waist, placing my head on her shoulder.

"In those heels, you're almost as tall as me," I whisper into her ear.

She cradles her right arm around my neck, leaning her head toward mine. "Almost."

Pivoting to face me, she adjusts my red tie and the lapels of my charcoal-gray suit. "Mmmm. Gorgeous." A glint appears in her cocoa-brown eyes as they roam over my body. "Whose idea was this party again?"

"Umm...yours, genius," I gently remind her, my cock hardening at the lustful look she's giving me.

She bobs her head up and down in realization. "Oh right."

I lean in closer, my lips grazing hers. "But save that look you just had in your eyes for later, baby."

Her tongue pops out to lick my lower lip. "I plan to, Harvard."

I groan in frustration. "Ugh. Okay, let's go greet our guests before I rip that stunning outfit off of you."

I pull Allegra by the hand and lead her out of the bedroom to our kitchen, where my mom is making her trademark salad with pears, walnuts, and champagne dressing.

"Hello, my darlings." She greets us with kisses and hugs. "Salad is just about ready."

The elevator *ping*s, and Allegra's father pops out carrying two shopping bags. *"Buon Natale!"*

Allegra rushes to greet him. "Papa, it's technically not Christmas yet."

"Well, this is a holiday party. So, *Buon Natale!*"

I can't help but smile at his enthusiasm, which reminds me of something. "Mr. Orsini, why don't you let the women handle the food while we have a talk in my office?"

"Yes, menfolk talk man things. Women stay in kitchen because women must provide sustenance for menfolk after discussing big, important things that women do not understand," Allegra declares in her best caveman impression.

Mr. Orsini walks ahead of me as I give a quick smack to my wife's lovely backside. "Smart-ass," I whisper into Allegra's ear as I pass by her.

Once we're behind the closed door of my office, I turn to my father-in-law, looking him straight in the eye.

"Mr. Orsini, Allegra has told me about your situation with your building, and I would like to help in any way I can."

He mutters something Italian under his breath before replying, "I know. My daughter should not have shared anything with you. This is my business."

I take a deep breath. "Please just hear me out, sir. I know how proud you are of what you've achieved with the shop, that it's a part of you. That's how I felt about my family's company. It was in my blood, started by my great-grandfather when he emigrated from England to make a better life for himself. And when I had to dissolve the business because of what my father had done, it nearly killed me. But it didn't because I had Allegra. She helped me through it. She made me realize that there's more to life than money."

"So you're starting over now."

"And it's been difficult sometimes, but it's getting better. I love business because I have a mind for it, and I'm good at it, which is why I'm not giving up."

He pauses before answering, allowing a quick smile. "Sounds like something I would've said all those years ago, when I took over the butcher shop from Sergio. I love working with my hands, talking to my customers. They're part of my family. *Mia famiglia.*"

"Which is why I want to help you financially. We can discuss the terms and draw up a contract if you like. Everything will be done on your terms. I could even become a silent partner in the shop."

Mr. Orsini's eyebrows dip in curiosity. "Hmm. That would be something I could consider."

"Then we'll talk about it more after the holidays?" I ask expectantly.

Silence, then my father-in-law nods his head. "Yes, I would like that very much."

He extends his hand to me, and I take it, shaking it firmly. "Excellent. I'm so pleased I can do this for you."

Mr. Orsini pulls his hand back, then pats my shoulder. "*Grazie*, Davison. I don't know what else to say. Just thank you."

I grin warmly back at him. "It's my pleasure, sir. Making you and Allegra happy makes me happy."

I hear more voices as we approach the kitchen. Tomas and Luciana are standing in the kitchen with Allegra, marveling over something in a plastic container.

"What's everyone freaking out over?" I interrupt them.

Everyone turns to me. "We're oohing and aahing over the plum dumplings that Tomas made," Lucy says by way of a hello.

"They're a Czech tradition," Tomas announces proudly. "You coat them in sugar, then you eat them."

"And this is also a tradition!" Luciana shouts, shoving her left hand in front of my face, her ring finger adorned by a sparkling solitaire diamond ring.

My eyes widen and my mouth drops at the sight. "Congratulations!" I kiss her on the cheek and shake Tomas's hand. "When did this happen?"

"Yesterday, and there's something else we haven't told you yet," Lucy hints cryptically. She looks at Allegra. "We're having twins, Alli!"

Allegra screeches in shock. "Oh my God! That is amazing!" The two best friends embrace as I pat Tomas's shoulder. "Well done."

He grins knowingly at my meaning. "Thank you, sir."

"Davison, please," I correct him, and he nods in return.

"I think it's time for some champagne," I announce, heading

out to the bar to pop open a bottle. On the way there, I turn on the CD player. Bruce Springsteen singing "Santa Claus is Coming to Town" begins to blare over the speakers.

Everyone gathers in the living room, with Allegra bringing in hors d'oeuvres on a silver tray, placing them on the coffee table. I pour a flute of champagne for everyone, and some club soda for Luciana.

"To my best friend and her fiancé and their impending arrivals!" Allegra toasts as we lift our glasses. "Cheers!"

Just as we take sips of the bubbly liquid, a *ping* emits from the elevator.

"Must be Derek and Aaron," Allegra guesses.

The doors open, and Ian steps out, with Ashton holding his hand.

Silence permeates the room.

Ian clears his throat nervously. "We were invited, weren't we?"

Allegra and I exchange looks. I take her hand, making our way over to them in the foyer. "Yes, you were invited," I reassure him. I look at them together. "So you *were* with him in Hong Kong?"

"She was," Ian confirms. "I hope that's not a problem."

"Not at all." I turn to Ashton. "Christoph raved about you when I spoke to him. I guess this makes it official."

"It does," Ashton replies in a strong, steady voice. "I hope you'll be happy for Ian and me."

An arm encircles my waist, a hand gripping my side. "We are, Ashton. I'm glad for the both of you," Allegra replies for the both of us.

"As am I," I join in. "Please come in."

Ashton hands a cake box to Allegra, who takes it from her and heads for the kitchen. Ian and Ashton follow me into the living room, where pleasantries are exchanged, though side eyes roam over the new couple from the rest of our guests, which doesn't surprise me in the slightest. I change the CD to Elvis Presley to lighten the mood in the room.

As I begin to head back to the kitchen to check on Allegra, Derek and Aaron arrive, with Derek declaring, "Let's get this party started!" as his husband rolls his eyes. I greet them as Derek looks into the living room.

"Davison, has the world ended or is that Ashton standing in your apartment?"

"That is her." I sigh. "Who would ever have imagined that?"

"Not me, that's for damn sure," Allegra declares, joining us from the kitchen. She pecks Derek and Aaron on their cheeks, then sniffs the air. She looks down at the casserole dish that Derek is holding. "That smells incredible."

"It's my *grand-mère*'s crawfish étouffée," Derek proudly informs us. "Now, Davison, lead the way to the bar, because I must imbibe *tout de suite*."

I laugh as they follow me to the living room, handing them each a glass of champagne. Lucy sits down at the piano and starts to play "Winter Wonderland," encouraging everyone to join in. Her attitude is infectious, and our guests surround her to sing with her, some in tune, other proudly off-key.

I glance over at the kitchen. Allegra stares out at us wistfully, then returns to doing something on the counter.

I slip away from our friends and family to see what's going on with my wife. I find her putting serving forks and spoons into the potluck dishes.

"I think we're about ready to eat," she whispers.

I take two steps to her, turning her away from the food to face me. "You okay, baby?"

Her eyes sear into mine as she nods. "I'm fine. I'm just…"

"What?" I ask gently.

Her eyes lock on mine. "Thank you for never giving up on me."

I cup her face, shocked at her admission. "I would never give up on you. That thought would never even cross my mind because I love you so fucking much. I will never leave you, Allegra. You're my wife. For better, for worse, and all that crap that comes with it."

Allegra laughs. "And thank you for always making me feel better when I need it most."

I kiss the tip of her nose. "You're welcome. Oh, by the way, your father agreed to let me help him with the shop and his apartment. We're going to discuss it more after the New Year."

A huge smile lights up her face as she grabs me in her arms. "Oh, Davison, thank you so much! I know he can be a stubborn ass sometimes—"

"Like father, like daughter," I mutter.

She shrugs her shoulders playfully in my embrace. "I know. I can't help myself."

I pull back so I can give her a quick kiss on the lips. "It's okay, Venus. I love you anyway."

She pokes me in the ribs. "Ha-ha. Funny husband. Seriously, though, thank you."

"Anything for you, wife." I look out into the living room. "I think we should serve dinner before Luciana and Tomas break into a rendition of 'I Got You, Babe.'"

Allegra sighs. "Knowing them, I think 'Let's Call the Whole Thing Off' would be more like it."

Sharing a knowing laugh, I pick up one of the serving dishes from the counter, turning for the dining room.

"Hey, Harvard," my wife calls out to me.

I look back into her warm brown eyes. "Yeah, baby?"

She gives me a quiet smile. "Love you too."

Chapter 20

Allegra

One year later…

The young female voice of a twenty-two-year-old opera student fills the cavernous room, doing its best to attempt what was once known as my signature aria, "Sì, mi chiamano Mimì" from *La Bohème.*

Except she's doing it all wrong.

"Claudia, stop," I demand of my student.

Five pairs of eyes focus on me, including Claudia's, whose eyes are more nervous than the others, as they rightfully should be.

"You're not understanding the tone of the aria. She's not going through a laundry list of her likes and dislikes. This isn't a first date. Mimì is poor, starving, and suffering from tuberculosis, and she is just moved that someone like Rodolfo is interested in her, not from a romantic standpoint but a human one. They're making a connection, and she is blooming because of it, like the flowers she is singing about, because they bring her such joy."

Claudia nods as I go on.

"You must feel the words. Place yourself in her shoes. Imagine if you were starving, you had barely any strength, but with one simple question from another person about your name, you open up—that spark of life is still inside you. Someone genuinely wants to know you. How would that make you feel?"

Claudia pauses a moment, then smiles to herself. "Pretty freaking happy."

I laugh in response, as does the rest of the class. "Exactly. Now try it again."

She clears her throat, closes her eyes, then begins again.

As her voice carries, this time much more slowly and with deeper emotion as I instructed, I close my eyes. Thanks to Signora Pavoni, I'm now working as an adjunct professor of voice at my alma mater, the Gotham Conservatory. I was grateful to her for thinking of me because I knew I needed something to occupy my time, and teaching has certainly filled the void of not being able to sing professionally. I do know that it's been a boost to the school, being able to boast of having a famous name on their staff, as famous as I was—that is, for a fleeting month. Others may have found that offensive, but I don't mind it because that's not my life anymore, and sometimes, I'm grateful for it.

A flutter of pain suddenly moves within me, my heart swelling at the memory of me singing this on the stage of the Met all those months ago, my dream coming true. But then I open my eyes and look down at the rings on my fingers, the ones that mark me as Mrs. Davison Berkeley, and I know that this is where I'm meant to be, helping others achieve their dreams of their own debuts at the Met.

Just as Claudia comes to a finish, I sense his presence. It is something my body is now attuned to, knowing when he is near me. I glance over at the door, and sure enough, Davison is standing outside, his emerald eyes blazing at me from behind the sliver of glass. His face softens when I see him, his entire face enveloped by an enormous grin. I nod, holding up a single finger to indicate class is almost over.

I applaud Claudia's performance, as does the rest of the class. "*Brava*, Claudia. Much better. Did you feel the difference?"

Slight tears escape the edges of her eyes. "I did. I really did."

"And that is exactly how I felt when the same thing happened to me. I just knew it. And it felt wonderful." I clap my hands together and rise to my feet. "Well done, class. Thank you, and I'll see you next week."

My students shuffle out of the room, with Davison holding the door open for them, ever the gentleman that he is, with a few female students giving him a breathless "Thank you" as they leave. I can't really blame them, because my husband is hot, but that's what I love most, the fact that he *is* my husband.

With the students gone, Davison shuts the door and strides straight to me, like a lion about to devour its prey. "Professor Berkeley, may I carry your books home?" His voice rumbles in that way that makes my toes curl and my core wet.

I take him into my arms as he folds me into his embrace. "Absolutely. And if you're good at it, we could make it a permanent thing."

His soft lips cover mine with a slow, deep kiss. "We already have, Venus."

"Just want to be sure you're up to the task, Harvard. Carrying a girl's books home is a big fucking deal."

"Mmmm," he purrs. "Love that smart mouth of yours."

He leans in to kiss me one more time before I break away from him. "I do have an office, you know."

"Lead the way, baby."

I gather my things, shove them into my tote bag, which Davison promptly takes from me, and lead him out the door. We walk hand in hand to the office I share with Signora Pavoni, my name, Allegra Orsini Berkeley, written on a piece of masking tape attached to the brass nameplate just beneath hers as a temporary fixture.

Once inside, I sit down on her leather couch, kicking off my pumps and stretching out my legs. Davison settles himself at the other end, taking my stocking-clad feet into his hands as he starts to rub them.

"God, that feels amazing, baby," I moan in relief. "You know what this reminds me of, of course?"

"As if I'd ever forget, Venus. Those long rides home in the Maybach after your shifts at Le Bistro, me taking care of you, something I look forward to doing for the rest of my life."

"You still won't tell me where you learned to do that so well, though."

"What can I say? I possess many talents. Besides, I think I like this look on you."

"Which would be?"

He looks at me, his eyes roaming over my body. "The sexy schoolteacher thing you've got going on. Your hair pulled back in a low ponytail, the black dress, stockings, the black patent pumps. It's hot, baby. I can just imagine loosening your hair as it falls down your shoulders, then fucking you bent over that desk, then—"

I hold up my hand to him, palm facing out. "Whoa! Hang on, there, Harvard. First of all, that's Signora Pavoni's desk, so that would just be wrong on all levels. And second, I probably won't be able to fit into this dress for much longer. In fact, you'll need to take me clothes shopping in a few months."

Davison's eyebrows furrow in confusion. "You've lost me, Allegra. You're not into all that, the shopping thing. That's not you."

I smile, my heart racing with excitement. "I know it's not, and you never have to worry about that. But I won't have a choice thanks to our baby growing inside me. The only things I'll be able to fit into are your Harvard sweats."

His eyes pop open, his jaw locking in shock. "What did you just say?" he asks, barely above a whisper.

I sit up, taking his hands and placing them on my belly. "I'm pregnant, Davison. We're going to have a baby," I announce in a calm, strong voice.

He clamps his lips together, trying to keep himself in check, but as tears start to fall from his eyes, his emotions overwhelm him. He leaps up and hauls me to my feet, twirling me around and around as he whoops and shouts in pure joy. "Yes! Yes! Yes!"

I laugh, but I start to feel queasy. "Baby, I'm getting nauseous."

He instantly puts me down, grabbing me by my upper arms. "Fuck! I'm so sorry. Did I hurt you? Do you need anything?"

"No, I'm fine," I assure him.

"How far along are you?"

"Just two weeks. I wanted to wait until I was sure before telling you because I didn't want to get our hopes up. I'm going to start researching ob-gyns."

Davison starts shaking his head. "Not without me, you're not. Your doctor is going to be Harvard-trained, both undergrad and med school, residency at Mass General or the Brigham in Boston, or Mount Sinai, Lenox Hill—"

I roll my eyes and clamp my hand over his mouth. "Okay, baby. We'll do it together. Team Berkeley."

"Team *Orsini*-Berkeley," he corrects me. My tears now fall more freely down my face from his correction.

"I love that, Harvard. Now you really do have a reason to carry my books home."

He wipes my tears away with the pads of his thumbs. "It seems I do." Davison pauses, staring into my eyes so reverently, holding my face in his hands. "I love you so much, Allegra."

"I love you more, Davison. Now take me home, because we have a Google search to do and a nursery to design."

Epilogue

Davison

Lake Como, Italy
August
Five years later...

Loud voices and laughter fill the wide backyard of our villa. Lucy and Tomas are engaged in a not-so-friendly soccer game with their five-year-old twins, Mimi (named after her godmother, Allegra's, signature role) and Marika (named for Tomas's mother). Each child has blonde pigtails flying behind them as they fight for the ball. Mimi and Lucy are exactly alike—feisty and sassy, while Marika is more like her father, quiet and introspective. Tomas has built himself an amazing career in opera, with quite the following. His good looks have made him the object of affection of loads of female fans, but Lucy is always there to ensure that they know that Tomas Novotny is off the market, sometimes reminding them in ways that one wouldn't describe as ladylike, but then, that's always been a part of Lucy's charm.

With August being the summer month when all of Europe officially goes on vacation, the Novotny family has taken up residence with us in our villa for two weeks before they head to the Czech Republic to spend time with Tomas's family. They now divide their time between New York and Switzerland, with Lucy more than happy to stay at home with the girls while helping to comanage Tomas's career.

A pair of tiny hands slaps my face, requesting my attention return back to him. My nine-month-old son, Jack, officially named James Davison Orsini Berkeley, is bouncing on my lap, wearing the FUTURE HARVARD GRADUATE onesie that his mother put on him this morning. Named for his grandfather Giacomo, whose name translates into James in English, Jack was a pleasant surprise when Allegra told me she was pregnant for the second time eighteen months ago. That was when Lucy educated me about the purpose of a "push present," something I had no idea about when Allegra gave birth the first time around. Apparently, a push present is something the husband is supposed to give to his wife as a token of gratitude for giving birth. I wish I'd known about this when Allegra had our first baby, because it had been a tough labor for her. It lasted twenty-four hours, and when the baby went into fetal distress, her doctor immediately performed a C-section to get the baby out, but Serena Concetta Orsini Berkeley arrived in this world screaming and perfect, her tiny head covered in dark hair. Now every time I make love to my wife, I kiss her C-section scar in awe and worship.

So, after our son was born, I inquired about the villa, this amazing place where Allegra and I had spent an idyllic holiday when she was training under the tutelage of La Diva all those years ago. It wasn't officially for sale, but for the right price, the owner was willing to give it up for me. I wanted this place for Allegra, no matter what it cost. It had been that way for me ever since I met her. I would do anything to make my love, my Venus, happy. After I bought it, I had the real estate agent who coordinated the sale send me the keys so that I could present them to Allegra, along with a picture of the villa. The day after Jack was born, I gave her both in a small box tied with blue ribbon, which caused her to cry buckets and buckets of tears, no doubt helped by her raging hormones, but I didn't care. She was happy, and that's all that mattered.

"Ow! Mommy! You're pulling too hard!"

"Well, that wouldn't happen if you would just stand still!"

I glance over at my wife and firstborn child from the lawn sofa where I'm sitting with Jack. Allegra is trying to fix our daughter's ponytail, which is now completely loosened thanks to her vigorous display of athleticism on the soccer field with her best friends, Mimi and Marika.

With her dark brown hair and round face, Serena is the spitting image of her mother, both physically and emotionally. But her name does not match her personality, because she is as far from serene as she could possibly be. She has a mind of her own and is just as stubborn as her mother. Jack, however, is more quiet, but still aware of what is going on around him. He takes things in slowly, while Serena is quicker to react. Serena is much more of a daddy's girl, because she knows she has me wrapped around her finger, as does her mother. The only part of me that Serena has inherited is my green eyes, while Jack has the deep brown ones of his mother.

My wife and daughter's loud conversation has now attracted the attention of my son, who is looking over at his mom and sister arguing about something as simple as hair.

"I know, son," I whisper to Jack. "Don't worry. We'll never be like that. We men have to stick together. You and me. Yankees games, fishing trips, I'll take you everywhere, even taking you to see the World Cup wherever they have it. I've got your back. But just one thing—you have to go to Harvard. I know that your godfather, Ian, is going to entice you with scintillating tales about life at Yale and do his best to make you a Bulldog, but that's not going to happen. Your blood runs Crimson. That's a Berkeley thing, and you're a Berkeley man. Nothing but the best for you. Deal?"

My son replies with a gurgle and more gentle punches to my face with his small fists as I laugh and plant kisses all over his sweet cheeks.

Allegra appears at our side and collapses on the sofa next to me. "Your daughter will be the death of me."

"Oh, now she's *my* daughter?"

She takes Jack from me, who instantly wraps his pudgy arms around his mother's neck. "Yes, because I plan to send her to boarding school the second she's old enough and stay home with my sweet boy," she replies in a teasing manner.

"Sorry, baby, but Jack and I just made a deal where we're going to do man stuff like sporting events and adventure vacations. No girls allowed."

"Ganging up on me already, huh?" She sighs. "I honestly don't know where she gets it."

I laugh out loud, doubling over from the shock of how oblivious my wife can be sometimes. "Are you serious? That's the best thing I've heard all day. I'm going to start calling you Pot instead of Venus, and our daughter will be known from now on as Kettle."

"She does not get it from me!"

I shake my head in amused exasperation. Allegra rises to her feet with our son. "Time to feed the young man. I'll be back after I put him down."

"I'll be waiting, baby."

"Better be. And make sure our oldest stays out of trouble."

"Easier said than done."

Allegra flashes me one last smile before she heads into the house.

The smell of baking pizza wafts over from the terrace. After we bought the house, I had an outdoor oven installed so we could enjoy fresh-baked pizzas during our vacations. I can hear Mr. Orsini saying something to my mother, then her amused reaction. Every time I ask her about her relationship with him, she contends that they're just friends, thrown together by circumstance since they share two grandchildren. But the more time they spend together, the more I think they're getting serious, which is fine with me, because after what my father put her through, I want her to be happy like I am.

It's been an amazing first summer here. We made sure that our family and friends knew they were welcome to visit us anytime. La Diva drives up from her opulent villa outside Milan for dinner at least once a week, once bringing Signora Pavoni as a surprise for Allegra. Ian and Ashton stopped by for two nights before they continued on their way to Greece, and Derek and Aaron stayed with us for a week after their holiday on Sardinia with friends. And even though we gave him the entire month off, Charles even visited us for a bit because he said he missed his family. Before arriving here, we also spent a week with Luca Montes, Allegra's former costar, and his family at their sumptuous villa on Majorca.

I take a long sip of my Peroni beer, watching my daughter fight like mad for the ball. I spot Allegra making her way back to me, lemonade in hand.

Once she sits down next to me, I stretch out my arm and bring her closer to me.

"Down for the count?"

"Yup, out like a light. Papa and Mona said they'd check on him in a bit." She pauses, then whispers, "I don't want to leave yet."

I snuggle her closer to me. "I know. We still have a few weeks, and this place isn't going anywhere. We'll come back as often as we can. But you have something exciting to look forward to, Ms. Artistic Director of Opera Education at Gotham Conservatory."

"It's so overwhelming. Class syllabi, committee decisions…"

"You can do it, baby. Remember how much you loved teaching that Puccini class? You were a natural with the students. Signora Pavoni knew what she was doing when she submitted your name for the position."

"You're right. One step at a time. There is a huge advantage to the position."

"What's that?"

She kisses me softly on the neck. "Summers off."

I hold my wife tighter to me. "Definitely. After reading the last quarterly reports for DCB, I might be able to take the entire summer off next year too."

My wife's head turns to me, her entire face lit up by her glorious smile. "Really? That good?"

"Better than good, baby. Better than I'd ever hoped possible."

Allegra wraps her arms around me. "Davison, that's amazing! I'm so proud of you. Why didn't you tell me?"

"I didn't want to get your hopes up, or mine, for that matter."

"We need to celebrate," she announces. "Once the kids are down tonight, I think we should head into town for dinner, and then take the long way home, like around the entire lake, and stop to take in the view."

"And would we do anything besides taking in the view, Mrs. Berkeley?"

She leans into me, her warm breath on my ear as she whispers to me, "Well, if we take the SUV and not your flashy sports car, we would have more room to do other things."

"But think of the fun we'd have trying to do those other things squeezed in so tightly together," I counter.

"Hmm...Love the way you think, Harvard. It's a date."

Allegra lays her head down once more onto my shoulder as we watch our daughter playing and laughing, her ponytail flying behind her.

I fucking love my life, all thanks to the woman cradled in my arms, her coconut-scented hair filling my nose with its irresistible scent as it did from the start, her curvy, luscious body arousing me now more than ever, making me desperate for dinner and our drive, when we will ravage each other like beasts, satisfying my craving for my wife, which never dissipates.

"What's wrong, Davison? You look so serious."

I kiss her hair to settle her nerves. "Far from it, baby. Just thinking about tonight."

My wife remains silent, simply holding me closer to tell me that she understands, as she always does.

* * *

Allegra

New York City. One month later...

Lying outside on a double chaise on the terrace of our new Tribeca penthouse loft, which we bought six months ago, a thin, cotton quilt covering us, we stare into each other's eyes. The sounds of the city envelop us, our strategy so that the groans and grunts when we make love will be swallowed up by the noise, as our children remain inside, Jack asleep in his crib and Serena coloring in her bedroom, impervious to what their parents are doing—trying to get in some sexy time before the end of Labor Day weekend and returning to our jobs tomorrow. Once we made sure the coast was clear, we snuck outside, turning on the iPod sitting in its dock so our song, "Avalon," could play on a loop while we made love.

Davison's rock-hard cock is sheathed inside me by my tight muscles. He starts to move, thrusting into me as I throw my head back. I will never tire of the feel of my husband pummeling me, his eyes blazing with his desire for me, his hot breath caressing my face as he urges me on.

I moan in ecstasy, which instantly turns him into a primal beast, biting down on my breasts, trailing his mouth up my chest to my neck, licking it and sucking on my flesh.

"Oh, Davison…" I exclaim in pure rapture, my fingernails digging into his back.

"That's it, baby. God, I love the sounds you make when I fuck you," he groans. "You make me so hot. And you're always drenched for me. Love your sweet pussy."

"Always," I whisper. "Always…Don't stop."

"You're going to come so hard for me, Allegra," he grunts as he reaches between us, feeling around for my clit. My body jumps in reaction to his skillful fingers, bucking under him as he rubs the swollen nub over and over. My pussy clenches him, and I moan in beautiful release.

Davison begins to pound into me. I love this. I revel in it—the pain, the soreness to come, knowing that I can do this to him, that I turn him into a savage with one clench of my pussy on his engorged cock.

The veins in his neck strain against his flesh as he comes, shooting himself into me until I absorb every last blissful drop.

We fall into each other's arms, my fingers trailing softly up and down his back, his heart beating against mine, our breaths panting at mutual speed.

"Fuck," he pants into my shoulder.

"Mmmm. Indeed, Harvard," I purr in reply.

Davison shifts to his side and brings me closer to him. He brushes my matted hair off my forehead, kissing it softly.

The warm look in his eyes melts my insides. It is a look of satisfaction and pure love.

"Thank you, Davison," I whisper.

"For what, baby?"

"For everything you've given me. For our children, for you. I've never been happier in my life. And you know what I love most about you?"

He smirks. "My drop-dead-gorgeous body?"

I smack him on the shoulder. "No, smart-ass."

He frowns at me. "I'm now officially offended, not just for that but because you say there's only one thing you love most about me."

I roll my eyes. "I'm trying to be serious here."

He kisses me quickly on the lips. "Sorry, Venus. Go on."

"Your respect for me. You always believed in me and encouraged me in my singing, and you never thought less of me when I lost my voice. You've always treated me like a woman deserves to be treated by a man, and for that, I consider myself to be the luckiest woman on the planet."

Davison visibly swallows in his throat. He takes a deep breath, then takes my face in his hands and gives me a long, slow, deep kiss.

When he pulls back, he cups my face so he can look me straight in the eyes. "I'm the lucky one, Allegra. I don't even want to think about what my life would be like now if I'd never lost that damn glove. My life is so much richer now because of you and the children you gave me. Gave us. And it's only going to get better from here, because you're stuck with me."

Tears fall down my face as I stare back at my husband. "Forever," I declare.

Davison beams in return. "Forever, Allegra."

The sound of a crying baby interrupts our moment of reverie, bombarding us from the baby monitor standing on the side table next to the chaise. Then, without fail, Serena's shouts coming through the screen door assault our ears. "Daddy! Where are you? I need you NOW!"

"Now, Daddy," I repeat, giving him a knowing smirk.

With a groan, we readjust our clothes under the quilt, throwing it to the side as Davison sits up and rises to his feet, giving me his hand gallantly. We stretch together, then fold into each other's arms.

"I'll take Jack. You take Serena," I instruct him.

"Meet you in the bedroom, Venus?"

I smile back at him, so full of love for my husband. "See you there, Harvard."

We give each other one last kiss and step through the patio door hand in hand, sliding it shut behind us as we head back into our home to tend to our beautiful, screaming children.

THE END

Don't miss the extraordinary romance of Lucy and
Tomas in Sofia Tate's new novella

CRAZY FOR HIM

Available Fall 2015

To see how Davison and Allegra's story began,
please turn the page for an excerpt from

Breathless for Him

Available now!

Chapter 1

Thank you. Enjoy the rest of your evening."

I watch as the last of the patrons don their camel-hair coats and calf-length sable furs. Before they leave, the owner makes sure to shake each of their hands. As they exit, the black velvet curtain that covers the front door swishes like a whisper against the marble floor, shielding the interior of the restaurant from the chilly November air. They shuffle their way out to begin the search for their town cars, a fleet of which stand outside on Broadway, engines idling, waiting to be claimed.

I'm standing inside my work space, which happens to be the coat-check room of Le Bistro, a restaurant that is an institution on the Upper West Side of Manhattan. Like Sardi's in the Theater District, Le Bistro is its equivalent, except it serves the opera buffs, cineastes, and ballet lovers of Lincoln Center. Its owner is Elias Crawford, one of New York City's most well-known restaurateurs, known for his charm, sophistication, and meticulous attention to detail.

Dressed in my standard uniform of a white long-sleeved blouse with French cuffs, black trousers, and black ballet flats, my dark brown hair done up in its usual chignon, I turn and take in my surroundings. Technically, my work space is a closet, lined with clothing rods for coats and jackets and shelves for handbags and briefcases. Since I began working there, I have checked an eclectic collection of items, from a famous rock star's red leather jacket pockmarked with cigarette burns to a vintage Louis Vuitton trunk that took up most of the traffic pattern.

Lola, the statuesque hostess, pokes her head in the door. "We're done, Allegra. You can start closing up."

I nod. I begin to wrap the plastic check numbers in an elastic band, stowing them in the shoe box that I use as a Lost and Found. I count my tips and tuck them into my purse.

As I take one last survey of the room, I spot two objects on the floor. One is a black-and-white silk scarf, the name HERMÈS imprinted in the lower right-hand corner.

The other is a man's driving glove, brown lambskin, cashmere-lined, with initials stitched on the inseam—DCB.

I stow both items in my Lost and Found shoe box. Perhaps the owners will collect them in the next few days.

* * *

"Did you hear about Davison's latest venture? He's flying to China to check out some new company that's doing amazing stuff with voice technology."

"Ha! 'Voice technology,' my ass! The only voice he's concerned about getting away from belongs to that shrew girlfriend of his, Ashton. She's got a hot body, but she's a total bitch—at least that's what I've heard."

That's what gossip is to me. Hearsay. It's common for someone to approach me while I'm working, offering me monetary compensation for any kernel of gossip that involves a celebrity. Because of its trendy status and location, Le Bistro attracts everyone from politicians to film stars to opera divas, basically anyone who's ever appeared in *Vanity Fair*. I knew since I began working here six months ago that if someone really wanted the truth about a scandal, the people to eavesdrop on were the doctors and lawyers who came into the restaurant. But I treat my place of work as a confessional; whatever I overhear will never be passed on to a third party.

The two men retrieving their coats are discussing the couple whose names and faces were featured almost every day on Page Six—Davison Cabot Berkeley, the Manhattan billionaire and heir to the Berkeley Holdings fortune, and Ashton Lane Canterbury, the heiress of the Canterbury family. Since they're the "it couple" of Manhattan, their histories are well known thanks to the tabloids and business pages. They're childhood friends. He has the proper pedigree: age thirty-one, prepped at Exeter, undergrad and MBA from Harvard, while she went to Miss Porter's and Wellesley.

A match made in WASP heaven.

It's funny, though, because every time I see their photo in the paper, she always looks much happier than he does, as if he would rather be anyplace else than with her. My life is far removed from the circles they travel in, but seeing such a handsome man so miserable with the woman he supposedly loves, I wonder if he is truly in love with her. I'm twenty-four, a butcher's daughter, but I don't envy their social or financial status in society.

I'm putting away the men's tips in my purse when a sharp knock on the flat ledge of the coat-check room's half door brings me back to the present moment.

"Excuse me? Are you working or not?"

At the door stands a tall woman with platinum-blonde hair that cascades down the back of her fur coat, a black crocodile Birkin hanging in the crook of her elbow.

"I said, did you happen to find a black-and-white Hermès scarf two nights ago?" her voice shrills above the cacophony of the restaurant. Her thin, oval-shaped face holds an exasperated look, while her blue eyes burn my face like a set of lasers.

"I did. Just a moment, I'll retrieve it for you."

As I pull out the Lost and Found box, I hear the woman speaking to her female entourage. "Oh my God, Davis is the biggest nerd. He never wants to go out. All he wants to do is stay home and read books or watch movies. He's *so* boring." She sighs. "But at least we're going away for the holidays to his family's chalet in Gstaad. I can't wait to see his new jet. We have invitations to *so* many parties when we're there."

Suddenly, I know whose scarf I'm holding. It belongs to the shrew herself, Ashton Canterbury.

Ashton's friends giggle in enchantment over the gilded life she is supposedly leading.

I walk back to Ashton with scarf in hand. I observe her, concluding that the tabloid photos actually make her look better than she does in person.

"Took you long enough," she huffs. "I hope nothing's happened to it."

"It's in pristine condition, madam. I kept it safe," I reassure her.

"Yes, well, it looks fine. Let's go, girls."

The lack of a gratuity from her does not come as a surprise to me.

* * *

"'O mio babbino caro'?"

Two days later during the lunch service, I'm bent over picking some dust off the floor humming the aria to myself when a deep male voice interrupts me.

I'm still distracted when I reply to the man. "Yes, how did you know?"

"My family has a private box at the Met."

When I stand up and turn to the door, I see in front of me what no photo could ever do any justice, now that Davison Cabot Berkeley is standing in front of me. He has to be over six feet tall, with dark brown wavy hair that borders on black. His eyes are deep green with flecks of amber in them. On any other man, his lips would look odd because of their lush shape, but on his chiseled face, they are perfectly suited.

He's dressed in a navy-blue wool coat, open to reveal underneath it a dark gray pin-striped suit and tie, accentuated by a button-down shirt in a lighter palette. A cashmere scarf the same shade as his coat is tied around his neck.

His eyes meet my dark brown ones, and in a flash, my throat goes dry. Shivers run up and down my arms. My pulse increases because of the way he stares at me. His head rears back slightly, and he takes in a deep breath through his aquiline nose. But it's the intensity of his eyes that paralyzes me. They sear me, as if they have the ability to read my inner thoughts without having to speak a word.

After a few seconds that seemed more like a full minute, I clear my throat. "You're very fortunate. May I be of service, sir?"

A small grin appears on his face. "Yes. I seem to have misplaced a glove. By any chance, would you happen to have found it?"

"I believe so. Could you describe it?"

"Brown driving glove, cashmere lined. My initials are on it. DCB. Davison Cabot Berkeley."

The sound of his voice warms my body, as if it were a cashmere blanket that tightly wraps around me. When he speaks, he speaks deeply, but it's more like a rumble, as if something is inside him on the verge of erupting. Even though he's only spoken a few words to me, I have a vision of him commanding others with that voice, and how intimidated I would feel, which is actually beginning to happen to me at that precise moment.

All I can do is nod my head. "Yes. I have it. I'll be right back."

As I turn to retrieve the Lost and Found shoe box, he says, "You have a lovely voice."

Thankfully, I'm looking away from him when he says that, because as soon as he does, my face turns hot. "Thank you, but I was just humming, sir."

"I can still tell, though. Are you a singer?"

My face now cooling down, I finally turn around. "Yes, I am actually. I'm a graduate student of voice at the Gotham Conservatory."

"Opera?"

"Yes."

"So I suppose the fact that you work across from one of the most famous opera houses in the world is not a coincidence?" His lips lift in a sly grin.

I laugh slightly from my nerves. "No, it is not."

He smiles at me. "Umm, may I…" he asks, gesturing to the glove in my hand.

I shake my head in embarrassment. "Oh, I'm sorry. Of course."

He takes the glove from me, running his fingers over the stitched initials. "Hmm. I wonder…"

"About what, sir?"

"I wonder when my parents named me if their goal was to see how many surnames they could slap on their newborn child."

I smile, laughing slightly. "I can imagine."

His head tilts at me curiously as he leans in closer to me. "What's your name?"

I swallow in my throat as his warm breath caresses my face. "Allegra."

"Allegra what?"

"Allegra Orsini."

He pauses for a moment. "That's a lovely name. Italian?"

"Yes, sir."

I look into his eyes, which are still boring into mine. I can't move. Something is…there. Something…powerful. It takes my breath away. We both seem to be stunned into silence.

He pushes back the tail of his coat to retrieve something from his pocket. He pulls out his wallet and shuffles through the bills.

A fifty-dollar bill appears on the flat ledge of the door.

I push the money back to him. "No, that's not necessary."

"Please take it. It's not just for the glove. It's been a long time since…I just want you to have it."

"Truly, I can't accept it. For the same reason."

He nods in understanding. He puts his hand over mine, the hand that's trying to return the money to him. He doesn't move, and neither do I.

Without warning, he begins rubbing his thumb over my hand, slowly. So slowly. My breaths begin to increase. His emerald eyes turn darker, hooded with a look that both scares me and arouses me. The warmth from his touch permeates my skin, setting the rest of me aflame. I can feel myself turning wet at the apex of my thighs. I press my lips together, determined not to break this moment. He is powerful and commanding. I can't look away. And I don't want to.

Then he moves in closer to me. His lush mouth opens to say something, his thumb still moving again and again over my hand.

"Do you think I could make you come just by doing this?"

"What?" I manage barely above a whisper.

"Answer the question," he commands huskily.

Before I can answer him, a cell phone begins to ring inside his coat, which effectively breaks the moment. I step back as he shuts his eyes, emitting a low growl, then pulls out the phone, grimacing when he checks the caller ID. He lets it continue to ring as he shoves it back into his coat.

He pauses a moment, then takes the fifty and returns it to his wallet. Like a magician, he then reveals the glove's mate from his coat, and I watch him put on both of them.

His hands now fully gloved, he looks at me again, both of his green eyes fixed on my own. They seem darker, ominous almost.

I swallow. "Have a good evening, sir."

He leans into my space, mere inches from me. His scent, something laundered with a hint of spice, permeates my nose, his hot breath caressing my face once more. "Good night, Allegra."

Once Davison Cabot Berkeley leaves, shaking Mr. Crawford's hand on the way out, I step into a corner of the coat-check room, leaning against it in the darkness. I press my head against the wall as I try to catch my breath.

No man has ever affected me like that before, mostly because I would never allow it. I know it was just a moment. That's what I tell myself. We will never see each other again. And it's just as well, because I never let a man in far enough to know my deepest secrets.

About the Author

Sofia Tate grew up in Maplewood, New Jersey, the oldest of three children in a bilingual family. She was raised on '70s disaster films and '80s British New Wave music and classic TV miniseries. Her love for reading started when she received a set of Judy Blume books from her aunt when she was ten. She discovered erotic romance thanks to Charlotte Featherstone. She loves both writing and reading erotic romance. She graduated from Marymount College in Tarrytown, New York, with a degree in International Studies and a minor in Italian. She also holds an MFA in Creative Writing from Adelphi University. She has lived in London and Prague. Sofia currently resides in New York City.

Learn more at:

SofiaTate.com

Twitter @sofiatateauthor

Facebook: Sofia Tate

Instagram: sofiatateauthor

Pinterest: Sofia Tate